Courtney's Collage

A novel

Sherille Fisher &
Barbara Joe-Williams

This book is a work of fiction. Names, characters, and places are used fictitiously. Any resemblance to actual events, locales, or persons, living or dead, is coincidental.

Copyright © 2007 Sherille Fisher & Barbara Joe-Williams

Published by:

[AP]
Amani Publishing
P. O. Box 12045
Tallahassee, FL 32317-2045
850-264-3341

A publishing company based on faith, hope, and love

Visit our website at: **www.AmaniPublishing.net**

E-mail us at: **AmaniPublishing@aol.com**

Printed in USA

ISBN-10:   097889376X

ISBN-13:   9780978893767

LCCN: 2007906154

Cover photograph courtesy of: **Istockphoto.com**

Dedication

This book is dedicated to the following:

**In Memory
Of
Rev. Annie Faye Fisher
1931-1998**

This book was written and completed while she was alive. She was a strong woman with a strong faith in God; a mother of nine children and an inspiration to many.

To my husband, Harrison R. Fisher, and our five children, Kelley, Dominique, Harrison, Jr., Jacob, and Joshua. To my parents, Johnny and Wilhelmina Williams; my big sister, Michelle; my close sister, Johnice; and to my baby sister, Natasha. To all of my aunts, uncles, cousins, nieces, and nephews, I wish I could name you all, but it is too many folks. However, I must name, my niece, Kyra; my husband, Harrison; my sister, Johnice; and my daughters, Kelley, and Dominique, who read my book and encouraged me to get it published. Thanks for pushing me until it was done.

Sherille Fisher, Author
****

Dedication

This book is dedicated to the following:

**In Memory
Of
Mrs. Ruby N. Sanders-Joe
1922-2000**

My mother has been the most inspirational person in my life. She motivated me to become the woman, wife, and mother that I am today. I would be nothing without her prayers. I still feel her presence everyday of my life.

To my husband, Wilbert L. Williams, and my daughter, Amani, I appreciate you both more than you'll ever know. Everything that I do is because I have both of you supporting me in every way possible.

And special thanks to our editor, Jessica Wallace, for her patience and red pen.

Barbara Joe-Williams, Author
****

Introduction

I am so glad this book is finally completed. I have waited many years. I started on this novel in 1991 while working in my husband's law office. He was the one who told me I should write a book. I have always loved to read novels and short stories most of my life. Since I am from a close family of only sisters, I decided to write about four sisters. I put a lot of myself in this book and after many years I found a publisher and a wonderful author to make my dream come true. Now I can put my first novel on the shelves with all the other books I have read. I am so happy and grateful.

Sherille Fisher, Author
****

I am happy to co-author this book with Sherille. She contacted me several years ago after reading my first novel titled, "Forgive Us This Day." Since then, we have become close and after she shared her dream of publishing with me, I was honored to work with her. I hope that you will be inspired by this touching story as much as I was. The materialization of this book goes to show us that we should never give up on love or ourselves. If you have a dream, you should see it through to the end because life is short, it's up to you to make it good.

Barbara Joe-Williams, Author
****

Chapter one

Courtney Marie Charles opened her sable eyes, quickly surveying her surroundings. The bed she'd awakened in wasn't hers. *How did this happen?*

Her head was aching and for a moment she started to panic. Then she remembered yesterday with all the great mid-term grades she'd made. That was why she'd gone to the Club Highlights last night.

Courtney was in her senior year at Fayetteville State University in North Carolina. It looked like she was getting her Bachelor of Science degree in Public Affairs after all. She was proud to be a part of the spring semester class of 1991. Courtney wanted to celebrate this achievement, but the few friends that she called had something to do last night.

So, she dressed in her finest clothes and dancing shoes and ventured out alone to the nearest club. When she arrived at Club Highlights, "Where Will You Go" by Babyface was playing. She looked around for a minute but didn't see anyone she knew. Sitting at the bar, she ordered a gin and tonic, heavy on the lime. Then in steps this fine black man with a familiar face.

"May I buy you a drink?" he offered. Courtney refused because she was already starting to feel woozy.

"May I sit beside you?" he politely asked.

"Sure, no one's sitting there."

After taking a closer look at him, she realized that he was also a student at the university she attended. Steven Palmer was his name, and according to what she'd heard, he had a good reputation.

Courtney was attracted to him as soon as he sat down. Standing about five feet eleven inches tall, he had ebony skin with a great smile, perfectly aligned teeth, full lips, and a well-kept mustache. He was indeed a good looking well-built man with sparkling dark brown eyes, nice thick eyebrows and lashes, and his wavy hair was cut close. Wearing all black attire, he looked like a handsome knight.

As Courtney lay in the full-sized bed looking at a sleeping Steven, she couldn't help but feel bad. She didn't remember much of what they discussed last night, but she knew what they'd done. By the time they arrived at his place she wasn't that drunk, just light-headed.

Steven and she connected so well last night, maybe too well. Her body was still moist from their heated actions. The passion was certainly there, and it had felt so right to be with him last night. *I wonder if the gin and tonic made the sex more exciting.*

He was so gentle. His kisses were so soft. He kissed her butterscotch skin in places she'd never been kissed before. Feeling the fire burning within her soul with every touch, her body ached for all he could offer.

The smell of their bodies mingled together still lingered in the room as the morning sun shined on them. Feeling a sudden mood change, Courtney's head began to spin.

Jumping out of bed, she ran to the bathroom fighting the urge to throw up. Once she entered the bathroom directly across from the bed, she dropped to her knees and released everything she had in her stomach.

Sitting on the cold tile floor beside the toilet, she placed her face into her hands and began to cry. Reflecting on her loose behavior, she felt ashamed. *Why did I let lust overwhelm me? Drinking like I did wasn't safe. I may not even be safe now. Where are my clothes? I need to leave now.*

Suddenly, Courtney felt someone's presence. As she lifted her head she saw Steven, the one who made her lose her mind last night, standing over her. Admiring his muscular shape, Courtney recalled how their bodies had blended together in harmony.

Steven was standing in the doorway of the bathroom with nothing on but a bath towel wrapped around his waist. At least he had something to cover his private parts; she was still nude. Steven reached his hand out to help Courtney up, but she refused it. After wiping her face with some toilet paper, she flushed it away. Standing up, she asked, "Where am I? How did I get here?"

He replied, "Courtney, you had a lot to drink last night. I picked up on it when I heard you talking. I didn't think that you should drive home in your condition."

Feeling the frustration coming over her, she said, "I think that we did more than talk by the look of things."

"Listen, Courtney, we had sex, and it was great. You just started taking off your clothes and got in my bed so I got in bed, too. I guess that the chemistry was there."

Courtney remembered having sex, but she didn't remember taking off her clothes. Some parts of last night were still a blur. Giving Steven a cold stare, she walked right by him in her nakedness.

Steven felt his body respond as she past him. He wanted her again and wondered if she felt the same. He desperately wanted to reignite the fire they'd shared. She was so sweet, smelling like fresh fruit. Her body was soft almost like a new born babe and the color of butterscotch candy. She had curves and breasts that seemed too large for her small frame and long black thick hair. Steven could look at her beauty all day.

Courtney suddenly felt dizzy as she walked towards the bed to retrieve her clothes. Sitting down on the side of the mattress, she eyed Steven as he walked over and sat next to her.

"Are you all right, Courtney? Can I get you anything?"

"I just need to lie down. I really feel sick."

"You're welcome to stay as long as you like."

"Steven, you don't have a lady friend who might pop up, do you?"

"I'm not dating anyone right now, Courtney. So lie back down and relax, okay?" Steven stroked her face and then kissed her forehead. He wanted to kiss her lips again but decided against it.

"Do you need something for your headache?"

"Yes, I think so."

He walked to the bathroom and returned a couple of minutes later with some over-the-counter pills and a glass of water. Steven also gave her a large t-shirt to cover herself. He was surprised at how comfortable she seemed around him. She was blessed that he wasn't a violent person. If she'd been in the wrong hands, she could be in danger right now.

Leaving the room with Courtney lying across his bed, Steven gently closed the bedroom door. Courtney raised her head looking around the room. She couldn't remember how the front of the place looked; she didn't even know if it was a house or an apartment. If she wasn't so sick she would leave.

Something about him made Courtney feel safe. Maybe the fact that they attended the same university eased her feelings about him.

Steven was a good guy from a respectable family, and had a good reputation at school, where he was admired by both the staff and the student body. His father, Dr. Samuel Palmer, was a respected gynecologist.

Courtney's family was pretty well off, too. Her father, Victor James Charles, was injured in an accident while performing his duties as a postal worker. The accident was with an eighteen wheeler from a major company. Fortunately, the trucker was at fault. After the case was settled, Mr. Charles was a very rich man. Courtney's mother, Diane, who'd been a nurse for ten years, retired to take care of her husband. The girls were able to get whatever their hearts desired.

Steven walked back into the room to find Courtney asleep. He couldn't believe he brought this woman to his place. *I wonder if she does this often.*

Remembering the horror stories his father had told him about having unprotected sex, Steven was careful about sleeping around. Being in good health, he donated blood twice a year. *I hope that she's as clean on the inside as she appears on the outside.*

Sitting on the bed, Steven watched Courtney sleep. He envisioned her in his arms while wanting to lie beside her. It was good to see that her hair was real since he hated weave. He'd spent most of the night running his hands through her thick mane.

Lately, the women he dated seemed so fake. Steven was just sick of fake hair, fake eye color, fake nails, and fake personalities. He could go on and on with the fake things that women put on their bodies. It was quite refreshing to know that Courtney didn't fit that description. She was a natural beauty.

At that moment, Steven thought about a girl from his past that died two years ago from heart failure. Catrina was real inside and out. He'd loved her with all his heart. There hadn't been anyone else like her. They'd dated two years before her sudden death. *Could Courtney be the answer to his prayer?*

The way he'd felt last night was better than ever. It felt so right. *Am I falling for Courtney?*

Steven left the room to fix something light for her to eat. About thirty minutes later, Courtney woke up. She lay in bed thinking about her sisters. She really missed them. Two of her sisters lived in Miami, Florida, and one was attending Texas Southern University in Houston. They would be astonished by Courtney's actions. Getting picked up at a bar really was very dangerous.

The fact that she had sex with Steven would blow their minds. Kimberly, the oldest, would tell her right off that she was being a slut. Jessica, who's a year younger than Courtney, would say, "You should be more careful, girl." But at the same time, she would want to know all the details. Majesta, the baby sister, would just want to know, "Why and how could you?"

Courtney's sisters were her best friends. She missed them so much and was looking forward to the sister reunion in May. This was something the sisters did every year or whenever they could. It started when Courtney went off to college. Most of the time, they met in Miami. That was a better location for their parents. This year they would meet in North Carolina since Courtney was graduating in May. She looked forward to seeing her family and friends.

It was the first of March, and Courtney really didn't have much time to plan for the big event. She was still disturbed by what she'd done. If she wasn't more careful, they'd be planning a funeral soon.

Courtney was in the bathroom getting dressed and rinsing her mouth out with a bottle of newly opened mouthwash. She hoped that Steven didn't mind her opening it. After washing her hands several times, she finally dried them off using paper towels.

Re-dressed in her black strapless dress and open toe heels, she pulled her hair back into a ponytail. Although she felt dingy, she decided to take a bath at home, if she could ever leave. Courtney felt like Steven wanted her to stay.

Hoping she could find her way back to the club to retrieve her car, she exited the bathroom. When Courtney entered the room, Steven was standing there with a tray in his hands. The stainless steel tray held grapes, strawberries, and a grapefruit sliced in half with a cherry in the center. He also brought her some ice water and a cup of decaffeinated coffee. "It's good to see you up and about. Are you feeling better?"

"Is that for me?" Courtney inquired, raising her eyebrows. She smiled at the pleasant surprise.

"Yes, you need to eat something. Can I take you to your car later?"

"Are we far from the club?"

"We're about three blocks away."

Courtney sat down on the side of the bed. Steven laid the tray on her lap.

"Steven, this is so sweet of you."

Sitting next to her, he watched Courtney eat the food he'd prepared. Although she wasn't very hungry, Courtney ate most of the light breakfast anyway.

"Are you gonna eat, too?"

"I'll eat something later," he replied. "Is Courtney your real name?"

"Yes, of course. I was too drunk to make up a fake name." Courtney knew that Steven was his real name because she'd seen him around the campus and had heard about him.

"I've never seen you before last night. But I would love to see you again. I'm sorry about what I did last night. It's not like me to pick up girls."

He paused for a second, looking down and then up again. "Courtney, I really don't want this to be a one-night stand. If I give you my phone number, will you call me?" he asked. After she responded with a nod of her head, Steven wrote his phone number on a small piece of paper and handed it to Courtney. "Take your time and eat. I'll take you to get your car whenever you're ready."

Steven left the room to watch television while Courtney finished her breakfast. Then she walked to the bathroom to freshen up and wash her hands again.

Feeling at ease with Steven, she believed that he was different from any guy she'd ever met. She just hoped that he didn't have anything she could catch.

Courtney had just come out of a relationship with someone, but it had been months since she'd had sexual intercourse. It had been foolish last night to have unprotected sex. Thinking that she really needed to do some praying, Courtney decided to walk to the club where her car was parked.

"Steven, thank you for offering to drive me, but I could really use the walk since it's only a few blocks away."

"Are you sure? I don't mind driving you."

"It's okay," she replied, walking towards the front door.

Steven followed behind her but stepped in front of Courtney to open the door. He placed a good-bye kiss on her lips as they stood in the open doorway. Then, his eyes followed her as she walked to the end of the driveway.

It was a clear Carolina morning with large houses sitting high on hills all along the street. Courtney remembered an accident that she'd had coming down one of those steep driveways. On that particular day, she was leaving a friend's house that just happened to be like the ones she was passing. Courtney decided to ride her bike down the driveway instead of walking. That turned out to be a bad choice on her part. She went down the driveway so fast that she lost control of the bike and ran into a cactus bush that was planted along side the driveway. Wearing a tank top and shorts at the time, she was left exposed and hurt.

Walking down the street, Courtney thought about Steven. *He's so fine and too nice to be true. I didn't expect him to be so polite.* At that moment, her thoughts shifted to Alex Reyes. He was a guy from her past that she'd dated in Miami. He'd left Courtney to go to Belize to take care of his ailing parents. In the beginning, they kept in touch with each other every other week. Then one day, Courtney received a letter saying that he'd met another girl. Alex told her that he'd met the girl about a month ago. Feeling like she'd lost a part of her heart, she stopped dating for months after that. Her plans were to attend the University of Miami, but after receiving that letter, she wanted to leave the state. That was the last time she'd heard from Alex. Now four years had passed, and Courtney still had deep feelings for him.

It was 1:30 in the afternoon when Courtney arrived at her car. Unlocking the door to her emerald green convertible Corvette, she slid behind the wheel, and drove straight home.

Taking a long hot bath, she soaped her body and rinsed off several times before exiting the tub. Courtney changed into her conservative work clothes and headed to the law office where she worked part-time. She wanted to look over some paperwork that needed to be filed. There were some personal letters she also wanted to read and respond to.

When Courtney arrived at the firm, Attorney Dawson Parker was in his office reading a newspaper. He always worked long hours including most weekends. He was an attractive man in his early forties with pale skin and dark blondish hair.

Courtney had started working in the law office during her sophomore year of college. One of her friend's from school, Nicole Carter, helped her get the job. She got along great with both attorneys, especially Attorney Parker. He was so cordial to Courtney and had often treated her to lunch. He'd even given her extravagant gifts, making her his right-hand girl.

Their relationship started a year after she had been employed with the firm a year. One Friday afternoon, Attorney Parker invited her to dinner, and she gladly accepted. They went to a seafood restaurant that was almost an hour away from the office. This particular restaurant sold conch, a delicacy of the islands. Attorney Parker had heard Courtney often talk about conch and he enjoyed it when he'd tasted some in the Bahamas while on vacation last year. The firm was doing well and the attorneys took several trips a year to unwind.

The attorneys' success was connected to a case that they'd settled for five million dollars about six months before they hired her. Courtney could hardly believe that she got the job. Her girlfriend, Nicole, really had put in a good word on Courtney's behalf. There was also a Caucasian guy working in the firm as a clerk when Courtney was hired.

On this particular Friday, the office closed early, around 4:00 p.m. Courtney didn't think they would ever get to the restaurant. As they entered the building, the waitress gave her a funny look. It was obvious that she knew Attorney Parker.

Looking around, Courtney noticed that she was the only person of color in the restaurant. The waitress looked at Courtney with an "I don't like the fact that you're with a white man" expression. However, she seated them and handed them a menu. Courtney was impressed because the menu didn't have any prices on it. She knew that it had to be an expensive place. She also liked the valet parking.

Courtney looked at Dawson with an uneasy expression on her face. He responded with a friendly smile. She noticed that conch was on the menu. She'd grown up eating seafood and loved it. The last time she had conch was in Miami. Attorney Parker remembered that Courtney liked it, and this was the only restaurant that he knew of that sold the delicacy. He planned to have some, too. The way they prepared it at this restaurant was great. It was cooked in a lemon butter sauce with mushrooms.

Dinner was delicious and Attorney Parker was a lot of fun. On the way home, Courtney asked him several questions about his private life. She even felt comfortable asking him about his love life. "Are you dating anyone?" she inquired.

"Yes, but she's out of town."

At the office, he'd never talked about dating anyone. He never got personal calls at the office either. Courtney liked his honesty, but she immediately changed the subject.

When they arrived at Courtney's place, she invited him in. He eagerly accepted her invitation into a spacious two-bedroom apartment.

Directing him to the sofa, she said, "Please have a seat." Then, she excused herself. Her bladder was full from drinking so much water at the restaurant. She rushed off to the bathroom.

Dawson admired the way that Courtney's apartment was decorated. She had beautiful artwork displayed and unique furniture. Courtney was a neat freak and her apartment was clean and well kept at all times. She had been diagnosed with a mild case of obsessive compulsive disorder (OCD) as a child. So she had to have certain things placed in a certain way in her room. Courtney liked things to be organized. Since she was worried about germs, she washed her hands many times a day. But the medication and therapy had helped her lead a semi-normal life.

Courtney was also excessive with collecting things. With a large picture collection, she had been collecting photos since elementary school.

Courtney walked out of the bedroom and asked, "Would you like a drink, Dawson?"

"No, thanks. I'm fine."

Sitting down beside him on the sofa, she studied his face. Gazing into his dark green eyes with an inviting smile, she let him kiss her hand and claim her lips with his own. Courtney could feel the hunger for sex just from his hot touch. They kissed passionately until Courtney stood and walked towards her bedroom. Dawson followed her with his eyes and body.

They didn't waste any time undressing each other. That night, Courtney and her boss sampled each other's bodies. It was a new and exciting pleasure for both of them. Being with a white man, an older man wasn't all that bad. He began to kiss her full lips and found that she tasted good.

Kissing her neck and shoulders, he inhaled her sweet fragrance. "Courtney, you smell delicious," he whispered again and again into her ear. Within moments, their bodies connected in passion.

Things didn't change that much around the office after that night. Courtney was still the dutiful secretary. She did her office work like always, not expecting any special privileges. There were some days when she and Dawson would make love in the office, but most of the time it was at his ranch.

"I love you, Courtney. And I want to marry you."

"I'm not ready for a commitment," she replied.

Courtney felt that she shouldn't be intimate with anyone else while they were dating, and Dawson felt the same. He loved Courtney with all his heart and wanted her to be his wife as well as have his children. Dawson didn't have any children, and he wanted a child that looked like Courtney. He loved Courtney's natural complexion.

After confiding in his partner, Attorney Robert Smith, about his feelings, Dawson was told, "It's not smart sleeping with your secretary." But he didn't care, he was in love, and trusted Courtney with all he owned.

He hoped that she wouldn't grow tired of him since she was so young and full of life. Dawson wondered if he had fully satisfied Courtney.

After months of being with only Dawson, Courtney decided that it wasn't fair to date him when she didn't want to marry him. Being that he was older, he wanted to settle down and have a family. Not only had he often talked about wanting a child within the next year, he already felt that he'd waited too late. Any woman his age would be too old or not willing to conceive.

Feeling that he was becoming too possessive, Courtney decided one day to break it off. It had only been two months since their separation and he'd never stopped trying to place himself in her life.

Desiring her so much, he told Courtney that she was still needed in the office. Courtney felt it was okay to stay with the firm because she could handle him since he always respected her wishes.

"Hi," Courtney spoke, passing Dawson's office.

He replied, "Hello." And then went back to reading his newspaper.

Courtney decided to organize the inside of her desk then type some important letters. This was "must do" work that could not be delayed. Since she'd taken Friday off due to testing, she was behind on her office responsibilities. But two hours later, her work was completed.

While Courtney was finishing up her work, Dawson called her into his office. She put her papers together and stamped the letters so that she would be ready to leave after talking with

Dawson. Upon entering his office, he asked, "How did you do on your exams?"

"Looks like I'm going to law school."

"Does that mean that I have to find another secretary?"

"Yes, it looks that way. I told you, I'm going to Thurgood Marshall Law School in Houston, Texas."

"Well, Courtney, it's going to be hard to find someone to replace you. You're an excellent typist, great with people, and you run the office flawlessly. Not to mention how you keep things organized around here. I'm going to miss those moments, your kiss, your smile, and those radiant eyes."

"Thank you," she replied, avoiding his stare. That was the best she could do.

"May I wine and dine you until you leave for Texas?" he asked, standing up, and walking towards her.

Courtney wondered what he was up to as he kissed her ever so gently on the lips. Then he pulled her into his arms.

Feeling the passion radiating from his kiss, Courtney pulled away from him. She knew it disturbed him to see that she didn't return his affection.

Stepping back, Courtney said, "Please don't do that again."

They hadn't been intimate for months and it shocked her.

Dawson sighed, realizing that he'd lost her; he didn't push it. He just stared at her with his piercing eyes.

Looking at his profile, his dark blondish hair showed hints of gray. Although he was in his mid-forties, he looked at least ten years younger. With a muscular body from college athletics and working out at the gym, he was an attractive man but just not the one for her. Without saying another word, he returned to his desk. Courtney left the building reminiscing about the night she'd spent with Steven.

Chapter two

When Courtney arrived at her apartment, she checked the mailbox. There was a letter from her baby sister, Majesta, who was also doing well at Texas Southern University in Houston. She'd just completed her freshman year. Her goal was to become a doctor since she was the brains of the family. She was also the prettiest child.

Majesta had done some modeling for department stores in Miami. Everyone always told her how beautiful her dark skin was. She never cared for her dark complexion but after being called beautiful black queen most of her life, she was beginning to like herself more.

Courtney's sister was writing to let her know that she was coming to help her pack for Texas. Majesta also mentioned that her boyfriend, Nelson, was coming with her. Courtney was pleased that her sister was coming but she didn't want Nelson to come anywhere near her. Nelson had raped Courtney and so far, Majesta didn't know the big secret. As a result of the rape, Courtney became pregnant. She never told Majesta. Courtney knew her sister would never believe it.

The thought of Nelson coming back to her place made Courtney sick on the stomach. It seemed like she'd just been raped yesterday.

It was Courtney's first year in college when Nelson came to North Carolina to check out the campus. He'd been offered several football scholarships. Nelson was older than Majesta and about a year younger than Courtney. He was preparing for college while Majesta was still in high school.

"Courtney, can Nelson stay with you this weekend so that he can check out the college campus?"

"Yes," she agreed. It was a favor to her sister that turned out to be a terrible mistake.

At the time, she really didn't know many people in North Carolina and it was a very lonely time for Courtney. But the last thing that she wanted was a visitor in her home, especially a man.

Nelson flew down one weekend and Courtney picked him up from the airport. It was a morning flight which was good for Courtney since she was an early bird. Nelson was looking good when she saw him. With a quick glance, he caught Courtney looking at him and could tell that she like what she saw.

It had been over a year since the last time she'd seen Nelson. When they arrived at the apartment, Courtney showed him around, and then he put his luggage in the hall closet. Once he was settled in, Courtney gave him a ride to the campus.

"Listen, I'm going back home to do some cleaning so I'll pick you up in three hours."

"That's cool," he replied, closing the car door.

Courtney returned home, cleaned up the apartment, and then headed back to campus to pick up Nelson. "I'm hungry. Is there somewhere we can get a bite to eat around here?"

"There's a burger joint on the way home. We can drive through and pick up something."

As soon as they arrived home, Nelson went to the bathroom and washed his hands. When he came out, Courtney went in and washed her hands several time before drying them off.

Thinking about her mild case of OCD, Courtney realized that she'd come a long way. She still couldn't stand untidy places; she still had to wash her hands more than necessary. All the guys she'd ever dated were neat freaks. They kept clean apartments and they all had great hygiene. She simply despised untidy people and found it hard to function in dirty surroundings.

Another problem she had was constantly checking things, like locked doors, appliances, and windows. Sometimes she would check the doors five times before leaving the house or going to bed at night. It made her feel crazy, but she couldn't help herself.

Thank God, I'm getting better with age. I'm glad that mama got me help early on.

Before Courtney could sit down, Nelson had wolfed down his burger. Noticing the mess he'd made, she began to clean it up. Nelson watched her cleaning up behind him and said, "You need to eat your burger before it gets cold."

Staring at him in confusion, Courtney continued cleaning knowing right then and there that it was time to lay down some house rules. A weekend with a slob was not appealing to her. "Listen, Nelson, as you can see, I keep my surroundings clean and in order. Could you please not mess it up? I don't want to see any more evidence of your presence. I can't stand untidy people, so don't upset me."

Looking at her, Nelson smiled as Courtney tidied up the kitchen. To him, it seemed clean. He couldn't see why she was making such a fuss. She looked sexy to him. It was hard to keep his eyes off of Courtney. When she finished, she put her burger in the refrigerator and went into her bedroom.

Nelson got up and turned on the television. He soon dozed off on the sofa. Courtney was also quite tired so she took a nap after she'd taken a quick shower. It was just before seven o'clock in the evening when she woke up from her sleep. She went to the living room and found Nelson still asleep with his shoes on the sofa. That was a big no-no with Courtney. Bumping him with her knee, she said, "Get up and go to the guest room."

He looked up at her sleepy-eyed and smiled. Courtney frowned at him. "I don't like people putting their shoes on my furniture."

Nelson didn't reply. He was too busy staring at her cleavage, noticing the swell of her breasts. *She's busty, pretty, and smart.*

Courtney, sensing his thoughts, went to her room and changed into something less revealing. She decided to stay in her bedroom and read a book. Reading was her favorite hobby. Courtney was almost finished with the book when Nelson knocked on her door.

"Come in."

Nelson entered the room and sat at the foot of her bed.

"What are you doing, Courtney?" he asked, trying to catch her eye.

"I'm finishing up a book that I started reading a couple of days ago," she replied, placing the book on the nightstand. She looked up at him. "Did you like the campus?"

"It's alright, but UM has a better football team."

"So are you interested in the academic program or the football team?"

"I'm interested in both, but I think I might go to Texas with Majesta. She's going to Texas Southern University when she graduates. I'll be there waiting for her. Courtney, have I ever told you that you're beautiful?"

"My sister is the beautiful one, Nelson."

"She is very pretty, Courtney, but you are beautiful."

"My sister has all the smarts."

"Listen, Courtney, I'm not going to beat around the bush, I've been checking you out. You're so fine, You know, you got me hypnotized. I would do anything you asked me to do."

Courtney replied using a stern voice, "Leave my room, Nelson, and close the door behind you."

"Come on, Courtney, stop playing hard to get. Majesta told me you love to have sex. She told me about the things you do with your legs. I heard that you are quite the double-jointed girl."

Nelson grabbed the bulge through his biker shorts. Looking at Courtney, he walked out of the room, closing the door behind him.

Sitting up in bed, Courtney tried to hide her excitement. She would have loved to show him a thing or two but he wouldn't ever look at Majesta the same again if she got a hold of him. *It would serve her right for telling all my private business. But it would still be wrong. Why did she tell him that, anyway?*

Picking up her book, she continued reading.

Nelson changed clothes and knocked on Courtney's bedroom door. "Can I borrow your car?"

Courtney really didn't like anyone else driving her car, but decided it would be a good idea for him to get out of the apartment for a while. *Maybe he'll stay out all night.*

So she quickly replied, "Yes, the car key is on the counter."

After Nelson left, she got some vanilla ice cream with sliced bananas. When she finished eating, she washed the bowl and tidied up the apartment. She checked the windows, the doors, and made sure all the appliances were turned off. This was something that she did every time she left her apartment or went to bed.

Courtney sat down on the sofa and turned the television volume to low. She wanted to hear Nelson's knock when he returned because he didn't have a key to her apartment. So she relaxed back on the sofa and started watching "The Late Show." Although it was one of her favorite programs, she couldn't fight the sleep for long. About one o'clock in the morning there was a knock on the door.

"It's me, Nelson."

Courtney jumped up and opened the door. Immediately she could tell that he'd been drinking. The smell of alcohol was strong on his breath. His speech was slurred when he tried to talk, leaning against the door frame.

"I can't believe that you were driving in this condition. You could have killed someone, or yourself," she stated, helping him inside.

He straightened his body the best he could, walked to the bathroom, and closed the door. Courtney went to check on the guest room for him. Then she returned to the sofa, waiting for him to come out of the bathroom.

A few minutes later, Nelson walked out butt naked. Not believing her eyes, Courtney blinked several times.

Nelson headed straight towards her, plopped down on the sofa, and wrapped both arms around Courtney. She tried to push him away with both hands but he was too strong.

Pushing her back on the sofa, Nelson started tearing at her clothes. There wasn't much to take off because she only had on a sundress and underwear.

Knowing that he was drunk and wasn't in the right frame of mind, Courtney became scared. "Stop, Nelson, please go to bed and leave me alone. You're hurting me!"

"Courtney, you know you want me, stop acting like that, sweet thang."

Standing over her with his knee on the outside of her thighs, Courtney saw a great chance to let him have it right between the legs. As soon as she got a shot she pushed her knee hard into Nelson's testicles.

Nelson fell backwards while holding himself with both hands, groaning in pain. Courtney got up, grabbed her clothing, ran to the bedroom, and locked the door. Nelson was frustrated and very hurt. He wanted to beat the crap out of Courtney but at the same time, he wanted to invade her body. At this moment, he wanted her more than he'd ever wanted Majesta.

Courtney was so scared that she didn't know what to do. She thought that maybe if she stayed in her room he would give up on this madness. *I just hope that he will go on to sleep now.*

No such luck. Courtney was on the floor beside her bed when she heard Nelson kick the door open. He quickly found her in the dark. Although he didn't hit her like he'd planned, he was still angry.

Sitting on the floor, Courtney felt helpless and was afraid to move. With tears flowing down her face, she begged, "Please don't hurt me."

Nelson had longed to have her even before he'd gotten drunk. Now he couldn't control himself, Courtney would be his tonight.

Feeling sick to her stomach, Courtney regretted that she hadn't called the police when she first entered the bedroom. *How could I be so stupid?*

Nelson stepped closer, giving her a lustful stare. "Courtney, can I just hold you? Lie in my arms and let's go to sleep. Relax, you're so tense."

"Nelson, get your black ass out of my apartment! I wouldn't sleep with you if you were the last man on earth. You are a poor excuse for a man. You're a mad man."

Immediately, he hit Courtney in the mouth. She could taste the blood seeping down her throat.

Throwing her across the bed, Nelson ripped off her underwear as she kicked and screamed. She wasn't going to easily give in even though her 110-pound build was no match for his six-foot-three, 260-pound frame. He was all muscles; Courtney felt like she was hitting a brick wall with her fists.

Finally, she stopped fighting and laid still crying. Nelson was too drunk to feel any compassion for her. Still tasting blood in her mouth, Courtney's body felt hot and bruised.

Realizing that he'd won the fight, Nelson smiled. In his blurred mind, he wasn't raping a woman. He was just getting what he'd craved.

Courtney screamed with pain as he forced himself inside her. This was the hardest thing that she'd ever had to endure in her life. Feeling her insides tearing apart, she closed her eyes and prayed for him to stop. The pain was so great, but obviously, Nelson didn't care. With the sweat dripping from his body onto hers, Courtney felt sick and contaminated. Directing her mind to another time and place, she imagined being somewhere else.

Moments later, she heard a loud moan from Nelson which brought her back to reality. He was finally done with his dirty work. All Courtney could think about at that second was Majesta. Her sister was responsible for this nightmare.

Courtney was sure that his actions would cause an unplanned pregnancy. She laid across the bed thinking, *He's going to pay for this. I can't tell anyone about this but I'm going to get him in my own way.*

Rolling over, Nelson went to sleep while Courtney thought about getting a knife and cutting off his manhood. But since her body was aching all over, she was too weak to move. After a while, she finally got up and took a steaming hot bath, remaining in the water until it turned cold.

Dressed in a sweat suit and tennis shoes, she sat on the sofa trying to stay up, but her eyes became heavy and she was asleep before she knew it. Later when she woke up, Courtney heard Nelson in the bathroom moaning and throwing up. She laid back down hoping that he would throw up his guts in the process.

Her apartment looked a mess; it looked like there had been a fight there. She decided to disinfect the apartment when Nelson left. His plane was scheduled to leave later that morning.

Courtney walked to the closet, got her gun, and waited on the sofa for Nelson to come out. She wanted to put enough fear in him so that he would wet himself. *If I could have gotten to my gun earlier, I would have killed him.*

Her mind was clear now, and all she wanted to do was put serious fear in him. As Nelson's head cleared, he felt sick and sorry for what he'd done to his girlfriend's sister. Looking at his reflection in the mirror, he said, "You're a jerk, man."

Although he couldn't remember everything that had happened, Nelson knew that he'd raped Courtney. Finding it hard to face her, he planned to sneak out as soon as possible.

Courtney was still sitting on the sofa waiting for what seemed like an hour before Nelson came out of the bathroom. Finally, she heard the door knob turning. Standing with the gun pointing at the door so that Nelson would be sure to see it, she yelled, "Don't move, you no good son of a bitch."

"Courtney, wait a minute. Listen, I'm sick, and you know that I was drunk last night."

"It was morning when you raped me, fool."

"I'm sorry, Courtney, please don't shoot me."

Pointing the gun at his head, she trembled with fear. Frightened almost to death, Nelson began to cry and beg for his life. That's all she needed to see and hear to satisfy herself. The rest would come later, she rationalized.

"Get your things and leave! You have ten minutes to get your ass out of here, or I might just change my mind about shooting you."

Hurrying towards the guest room, Nelson got his clothing packed and was out the door. Courtney locked the door behind him and checked all the windows several times. She spent two hours cleaning her apartment. Then Courtney took another bath because she could still smell the scent of Nelson on her body. She also threw away her linen and every dish that Nelson had touched.

I know that I'll need to see a psychologist as soon as possible to deal with this terrible experience. This whole ordeal is probably going to multiply my problems even more, she thought, hanging her head in despair.

Luckily, that was the last time Courtney had seen Nelson and that was over three years ago. Just the thought of seeing him again soon gave her a sick feeling.

Feeling confused about her life, she'd begun taking antidepressant medication again. Her doctor had prescribed it after telling Courtney that many people suffer from mental depression and never seek help.

Courtney could feel a change in the way she handled situations when she took the medicine. Things wouldn't get her down and the medication helped her to let things go sometimes. After being on the medicine for a year, the doctor took her off of it and she stopped going to the doctor. Courtney felt that her condition was much improved; she could cope with life.

Placing Majesta's letter on the dresser, she looked for Steven's number. Courtney needed to see him and longed for his presence.

When she called Steven, he sounded as if he'd just woken up. "Hi, may I speak to Steven?"

"This is he."

"Hi, Steven, this is Courtney. Remember me?"

"Of course I remember you. It's good to hear from you. I'm glad you called."

Courtney was happy to hear that. The last thing she wanted was to bother him. "Would you like to go to a movie?"

"Yes, I would. What time did you have in mind, and what time do I need to pick you up?"

"How about a six o'clock showing? You can pick me up at my apartment a little after five."

Courtney gave him her address and began looking for something casual to wear. Taking a long shower, she washed her hair, and pulled it up into a ponytail. She'd planned to cut it but she just hadn't gotten around to it yet. *I wonder if I called Steven too soon. We just met last night. Oh, well, he told me to call him sometime and I did.*

Slipping into a pair of blue jeans and a white blouse, Courtney lightly applied make-up to her smooth complexion. Then she tidied up her apartment even though it was already clean enough to eat off of the bathroom floor. All of the rooms were equally clean. Her pantry was filled with every cleaning item she could think of including carpet cleaner, fresheners, potpourri, and incense.

Everything was in order. She also changed the furniture around every two months. And she changed the dishes to different kitchen cabinets whenever she moved the furniture.

Around 4:30 that afternoon, Steven knocked on her door. He was certainly excited about seeing Courtney again, and she felt the same about seeing him. "Would you like a soft drink?" she asked, escorting him inside.

"No, I'm cool. Are you sure you want to go to the movies?"

"Yeah, aren't you?"

"Well, I was just thinking that maybe we could stay here and get to know each other better. What do you think?"

Courtney smiled at him thinking that maybe he was just too good to be true. He smelled good and had sparkling white teeth. She remembered how clean he kept his apartment and how good it smelled. "I think that's fine. We can stay here and talk."

They sat close together on the sofa. "Courtney, I didn't think that you would call me."

"You were so nice to me this morning; I just had to see you again."

"I'm glad you called me so soon."

"I just feel blessed. I believe that our meeting was fate, Steven."

"All I know is that I've been waiting for a girl like you."

Courtney blushed, looking deep into his dark brown eyes. Both their faces inched forward until their lips connected like magnets. Courtney felt herself melting into his warm arms again. This time she was in her right mind and what she was feeling didn't have anything to do with alcohol.

Steven kissed her passionately, holding her in his arms like she was the dearest thing in the world to him. Feeling his heart beat with desire, she could feel the longing that he had for her. Courtney returned his kiss like she wanted it to last forever. Then he whispered, "I need you again."

The warmth from her body and the racing of her heart made it difficult for Courtney to speak. Steven knew from the look in her eyes that he could have what he desired. Courtney stood up, leading him to her special room.

The room contained thirty framed photographs, twenty-five photo albums, and six picture collages, including one poster size collage. Each collage had a title. She had a family collage, a collage with baby pictures of herself and her sisters. It was the most beautiful collection of photographs Steven had ever seen. He was very impressed. That one room told him a lot about Courtney.

"Did you do all this yourself?"

"Yes," she replied, flashing a big smile.

She loved pictures and had been collecting photographs for many years. Every photo book was neatly organized and labeled. Each framed picture was neatly placed on the shelf or a wall. There wasn't any dust in this room or the rest of the apartment. She was a clean freak, just like him. This made Steven even more attracted to his newfound friend.

Reaching out for Courtney, Steven continued what they'd started in the living room by placing a soft kiss on Courtney's lips. She rapidly returned the fire. Touching the bulge in his pants, Courtney guided him to the plush carpeted floor. By now, going to the movies was long forgotten.

Steven moved his kisses down her neck as his hands found her breast. Courtney could see from the glee in his eyes that he was enjoying the feel of her body. She got up and retrieved a quilt from the closet. They both stepped onto the quilt and began undressing each other, one admiring the other's body.

Minutes later, Steven laid on his back and pulled her close to his side. He wanted Courtney to be at his side, to be his companion. She was feeling love for him already, and his lovemaking had everything to do with it.

There was a certain gentleness about him. *Could he be the one for me? Will the longing for Alex ever stop? If he called at this moment, I would probably go back to him. So how could I really be falling in love with Steven? Maybe it's just a sex thing.*

Around midnight, Steven left. Even though Courtney wanted him to stay, she didn't say it or show it. "I enjoyed your company. I hope that we can see more of each other."

"Me, too," he responded, giving her a long kiss on the lips. Courtney felt a warm flow escape her, and she wished he would work his magic all over again before leaving.

Looking in her eyes, he said, "I have strong feelings for you." Courtney just smiled. She wasn't ready to express her mixed feelings towards him.

Chapter three

Kimberly prepared her boys' lunch for school, and then she sat at the kitchen table, reading the Miami Herald newspaper. She got up at six o'clock every morning to get the boys off to school. Since Kimberly was the owner of her own business, she didn't normally go in until noon.

Hair and make-up is what she'd always wanted to do. And she did plenty of practicing on her three sisters. Courtney was always so concerned with her looks that her hair and clothes had to be perfect. She didn't let Kim just do her hair any kind of way.

When Majesta was modeling for a local department store, sometimes Kim would offer her talents regarding hair and make-up. Eventually, she turned out to be quite the business woman. Her beauty shop, Kim's Place, was one of the best in Miami.

Thanks to their parents, the girls had an opportunity to do whatever their hearts desired. The sisters wore the finest clothes. They all loved jewelry and lots of it. Even before their father's accident, they had the best things in life. But after the case was settled and he was awarded money for his pain and suffering, they had stuff they didn't even need.

Of course, they had a hard time in school with both white and black girls. The girls at school were jealous of them because they dressed well and they were also very beautiful. Kimberly had a temper and would fight in a minute. She wasn't concerned with what people thought of her.

One day, Angel, a big bully, tried to cut Kim's long, wavy hair. Kim was dressing for physical education class when she noticed Angel glaring at her. Apparently, the girl had an issue with Kim. So out of curiosity, Kim asked, "Is there a problem here?"

"I just can't stand girls who think that they're better than the next person."

Then Angel was joined by another girl, and Kim noticed they were the only people in the locker room. Kim, now disturbed by this situation, said, "Look, I don't want any trouble."

What she said didn't matter to either of them. Angel, the girl who started the trouble, suddenly pulled out a pair of sharp scissors and tried to cut Kim's hair. The way Kim knocked the scissors from the girl's hand and then punched her in the face surprised them both. Kim jumped on Angel and beat her silly.

The other girl went to get the coach because she thought that Kim might kill her friend and her too, if she interfered. Eventually, it took two physical education teachers to pull Kim off of Angel.

Once Kim was able to tell her side of the story, Angel was suspended for five days while she was suspended for only two days. Her parents were angry, but they understood.

Kim didn't have any more trouble with anybody after the news got out that she was crazy. She and her sisters earned excellent grades in school and Kim was chosen prom queen in her senior year.

Jessica was into track and field so she didn't dress up like her sisters. She wore comfortable casual clothes, tomboyish fashions. It was hard for her mother to get her to wear dresses until she was in high school. The baby girl, Majesta, and Courtney were into modern dance and tap. All of the sisters were talented. They sang in the church choir, but Courtney had the prettiest and strongest voice. She often led songs at church.

Kim started attending beauty school while she was still in high school. After falling in love with a Jamaican guy, Carlton Robertson, they got married as soon as she graduated. Her first son, Carlton, Jr., was born six months later. When Carlton, Jr., was two months old, she became pregnant with twins, Blake and Drake. Four years later, she had Jeremy. Shortly thereafter, she had a tubal ligation.

At twenty-five-years-old, Kim was the mother of four boys. Her husband became a dentist with a successful practice. Thanks to her parents, Carlton was able to go to college and not worry about working while in college. They lived in a large housing community in Cutler Ridge, Miami. Kim loved living close to her parents.

By the time Kim finished reading the paper it was 6:30. She woke up Carlton, Jr. and the twins for school and helped them get dressed.

Minutes later, she had prepared malt-a-meal and toast for their breakfast. The twins and Junior played well together, but there were times when the twins would double team their brother. Once the boys finished breakfast, it was time to catch the bus. They kissed Kim and walked to the bus stop.

Looking out the window, Kim watched them like she always did until they were gone. Jeremy was still asleep, so she cleaned up and wrote out a grocery list.

By the time she finished her list, Jeremy was awake. Within minutes, she had him fed and on his way to daycare because she wanted to go to the store before going to work.

While she was in the store, she saw Alex, Courtney's ex-boyfriend. Kim wasn't surprised that he asked about her sister.

"How's Courtney? When is she coming to Miami?

"Oh, she'll be here next year. I heard you got married, Alex."

"No, it didn't happen. We decided that we were not ready for marriage, so we broke up."

"You know, my sister was really hurt over you breaking up with her. She's been a different person ever since then. Courtney really loved you, Alex. I believe that she still loves you, but she won't admit it."

"Well, Kim, I thought I was in love with this girl, but then I guess I still love Courtney. That's really why I didn't get married. I've been thinking about her a lot lately. I want to talk to her."

"Alex, just pretend like you didn't see me today. If you want to reach her, you're on your own. I was surprised and upset at how you dropped my sister. Courtney wouldn't eat and she just stayed at home for months. I'm not getting involved in this."

"If I give you my number, will you please tell her to call me?"

"I said I'm not getting involved in this, Alex. I have to go to work."

Walking away, Kim refused to take the number. She finished her shopping and went home to drop off the groceries. It was 11:30 when she arrived home, so she called the shop and found out that it was very busy. Black women believed in getting their hair done. She even had a group of welfare moms who came in the first of every month to get the latest styles.

Braids were the only thing that she had on her schedule for today. She would do two heads which would take most of the day. The shop opened at 10:00 a.m. and closed at 10:00 p.m., six days a week. It was in the Miami Mall so she didn't mind being open late because security would make sure she got to her car.

When she arrived at the shop, she put on her apron and got started with the braids. Just from looking at her client's short hair, she knew it was going to be a challenge. First, she needed to wash and condition it. Most of the time, Kim had her hair washer to handle this. But today, the girl was so busy that she did it herself.

Kim really needed more help at the shop. A guy had come by yesterday to apply for a position. After reviewing his application, she decided to hire him. He was just what she needed in the shop. He had a clientele from working at another salon. She was sure that they would follow him if he was any good. De'won was quite a handsome fair-skinned man with soft curly hair cut into a fade. He was well-groomed and very articulate. And it was evident that he was gay because he said it in several ways. But he was such a riot.

They talked for almost an hour during the interview. Kim promised to call him before the end of the week. She decided that De'won would take Lisa's place. Lisa had made some big mistakes. She had her priorities all mixed up. Her last mistake had pinched Kim's nerves.

Lisa put a relaxer on a client's hair and left it on too long. The lady's face turned red, and she had chemical burns on her scalp. Kim had told all her employees not to book clients too close together. Lisa was working on too many heads that day and that's why she messed up. She'd forgotten about the client with the relaxer.

Kim told the poor lady that she would do her hair free of charge for the next five appointments. That included washing, setting, and some hair treatment solutions. She told the lady that she wouldn't need a relaxer until her hair was repaired. Then Kim told Lisa not to come back to the shop because this wasn't the first time that she'd had an unsatisfied customer.

Two days had passed since that incident. Kim decided to call De'won to see if he was still interested in the position. She talked with Lisa but determined that it was bad for business to keep her employed there. The business was doing well and Kim wanted it to stay that way. She wasn't going to let careless mistakes ruin her shop's name.

Kim finished the last client's head at nine that night, and arrived home around 10:30. Carlton had picked the boys up from daycare like always. They all ended up at the same place by the end of the day because the daycare picked up the older boys from their schools.

Carlton was a great cook and he loved cooking. When Kim arrived home, she smelled dinner. "Umm, it smells great in here."

She noticed Carlton in his favorite chair sleeping. Kim tipped over and placed a kiss on his cheek. He blinked his eyes open as she said, "Honey, I'm home."

Carlton smiled up his wife, stretching out his arms as he yawned. Then Kim went into the kitchen. He had made fried conch with lemon and shrimp fried rice. This was something he could have prepared on a daily basis for Kim since she loved it that much.

Kim and her sisters enjoyed dishes such as conch salad, fried conch with lemon, conch fritters, conch soup, and conch smothered in gravy. The sisters were raised on all kinds of seafood. Their father was also a great cook. Since he was handicapped, they had to redesign the kitchen to meet his needs. Mr. Charles had a stove low enough for him to cook on while in his wheelchair.

Miami is a good place to meet all kinds of people, and eat different kinds of food. The sisters loved Cuban food and spoke Spanish very well. Majesta had dated a Haitian guy and he taught her the French language. Courtney's first love, Alex, was from Belize. Carlton still had his strong Jamaican accent.

Entering the living room, Kim said, "I'm going to take a bath, honey."

"Hon, you not gonna eat your supper?"

"I'm so sleepy and my feet hurt. I'll eat when I get out of the bathtub, okay?"

Carlton went to the kitchen. He took some food out for Kim and put the rest away. Then he placed the dirty dishes in the dishwasher and turned it on.

He heard the telephone ringing and answered. "Hello?" He recognized Jessica's voice.

"Hi, Carlton, can I speak to Kim?"

"Sweetheart, she's taking a bath."

"Well, just tell her to call me."

Later on, Carlton gave Kim the message and she called her sister back. She ate dinner and spoke with Jessica at the same time.

"What's up, sis?"

"Kim, I got some bad news, girl."

All kinds of thoughts came rushing into Kim's mind. She pushed her food to the side and asked, "What's wrong?"

"Someone told Majesta that Nelson and Courtney had sex."

"That's a lie, Jessie. He knows good and well that he raped Courtney. She would never lie about something like that."

"Someone told Majesta that Nelson was bragging about sleeping with her sister in North Carolina."

"I knew this mess was going to hit the fan sooner or later. Courtney should have turned him in when he raped her. She didn't want to hurt Majesta's crazy butt."

Kim remembered how Nelson had tried to flirt with her when she first met him. "I think that we should call Majesta to see how much she knows and what she believes. Jessie, who told you?"

"Momma told me today. She said that Majesta called her crying about Nelson cheating on her and then she said that she's four months pregnant."

"What! I can't believe that Majesta let that happen," Jessie said, releasing a sigh. "It might be best to contact poor Courtney."

"Yeah, then we can get Majesta on the line next. We can't let that no good jerk come between our sisters." Kim put Jessie on hold and called Courtney.

It was raining extremely hard in Fayetteville. Courtney had been sleeping for about two hours when her sister called. "Hello," she mumbled.

Then Kim clicked Jessie back on the line. Now the three of them were connected over the telephone.

"Hi, Courtney. It's Jessie and Kim. Did we wake you, sis?"

"Yes, but that's all right. What's up?"

Kim spoke first, breaking the news to her sister. Courtney felt hot, she turned red with rage and her ears were burning. "That jerk is lying. He raped me, and he makes me so sick. I could just throw up right now. I should have killed him when I had the chance."

With tears rolling down her face, Courtney thought of Majesta being upset with her. There was silence across the line. "Courtney, are you all right, honey? Say something," Kim begged.

"I'll never get over the rape, but like I told you before, I do kinda feel responsible for it."

"Listen, Courtney, he didn't have to rape you. You said that you tried to fight him off. It's not your fault. You didn't invite him to your place. Majesta begged you to let his lazy butt stay with you. She knew he was a flirt. I told her when he tried to mess with me. I wish you would have shot him and told Majesta what happened, and then she wouldn't be pregnant with his baby today." Jessie was disgusted with the whole situation.

"I know, Jessie. I just feel awful. I thought this was behind me and now this. I haven't been sleeping with my boss. I don't think about Alex anymore. I've been trying to do better regarding relationships."

"Listen, Courtney, Kim and I are going to call Majesta. We'll start talking about our sister reunion to see what kind of reaction we get."

"That's right," Kim chimed in. "You need to get some rest. Don't worry yourself over this. Jessie and I will fix everything, even if we have to break Nelson in the process."

"Thank you. Please tell Majesta about that horrible night. I don't want to keep it from her any longer." Courtney thought about calling a talk show and telling the whole world about this mess, but she didn't have the guts. "Nelson had the impression that I was an easy lay. Majesta told him everything about me."

"Don't worry, sis. Jessie and I are going to call Majesta. We'll call you back tomorrow."

Chapter four

Courtney woke up at six o'clock the next morning wishing that the call she'd gotten from her sisters was a dream. She had an upset stomach and needed some antidepressant medication or anything to get her through the day.

With the answering machine turned on, she was screening every call. She knew that she wasn't ready to speak with Majesta today. There was too much to do. But first, she needed to start packing her things for the move to Texas. *I wonder how my baby sister feels about me now.*

Courtney would miss Steven. All this time they'd been going to the same college and now they get close during her last semester of undergrad. If she wasn't going to law school in Houston, she would stay. But this was her life's dream. She and Steven weren't serious enough for her to drop everything. *That's life.*

The phone rang while Courtney was washing her face. Walking to the living room, she listened to her greeting, and then the caller. Steven's voice came on the machine, and she picked up the phone. "Hello."

"Hi, Courtney, are you busy?"

"No, I'm never too busy for you."

With so much on her mind, she needed to talk to him again about moving to Texas. After making small talk, Steven asked, "Are you free for dinner this evening?"

"Ahh, I'm going to the office to pack up some things. Maybe you could come over here around five."

"Would you like to go to church with me in the morning? I'm a member at Antioch Baptist Church."

"Let's talk about it over dinner."

"All right, I'll see you later."

Both attorneys were at the office when Courtney arrived. Dawson had her check on his desk waiting for her. Courtney didn't expect to get paid until Friday, so this was a pleasant surprise.

She noticed that her replacement was coming in on Saturday to get started. Attorney Smith asked, "Courtney, would you help train the new girl?"

"Yes, sir, I'd be happy to."

"Good. We're planning to take you to have a farewell lunch on Friday."

Courtney showed Rita, a red-headed slim thirty-two-year-old woman how the files were color coded. She showed her all the forms, and gave her keys to the file cabinets. Courtney even told her about how each attorney liked his work to be done.

"You need to be on top of your typing, but you will be working on the computer most of the time. Just keep the files neat and never let the attorneys find any information not belted down. Always complete the case notes when working on a file. Try not to make personal calls when the attorneys are in the office. If they don't want to talk on the phone, you need to think of a good excuse to tell the client. Our clients tend to call quite often, so try to let them know how busy the attorneys are. Well, that should get you started."

"Thanks for the advice. I'm still nervous about working here. I feel like I can't do this alone. Did you have anyone else working in the office with you?"

"There was a clerk for a while, but it's been just me for a long time. I'm going to law school, so I spend lots of time in the office even when I'm off the clock."

Rita simply nodded as Courtney continued.

"Attorney Parker offered me a position in the firm when I pass the bar examination. But that's so far in the future; I don't want to think about it. You'll be all right when you get used to your workload. I was the first black person to work in this firm. It made me want to show them that I was just as good as any other person they could have hired. Oh, well, Rita, I have a lot to do. I'll be seeing you again before I leave town."

Courtney finished packing her belongings. "Attorney Smith, I'll see you on Friday," she stated on her way out.

On the way home, she stopped by the Piggly Wiggly for the ingredients for the dinner she was preparing for Steven. She decided to buy liver pudding since Steven had told her that he loved it. Liver pudding was a popular dish in North Carolina. She also picked up some dinner rolls, lettuce, and tomatoes for a tossed salad. Cooking was something that Courtney loved.

When she finally made it home, she cleaned up the kitchen and started dinner. Then, she took a shower and put on the sexiest black dress that she owned.

Courtney wanted to discuss the future with Steven, and she hoped that they could keep in touch when she left for Texas. Steven showed up at 5:15 p.m.

"Hi, would you like a glass of wine?"

"Sure, that would be nice," he replied, eyeing the low-cut mini dress with most of her breasts exposed. He wanted to control himself, but Steven couldn't keep his eyes off her chest.

"Do you like the liver pudding?" Courtney asked after they'd taken a few bites.

"Yes, yes, it's very good. It's been a long time since I've had this. I fell in love with liver pudding when I first tasted it as a child. They served it at school, and at restaurants, and my mother made it almost every week. But it's been over a year since the last time I had it."

"Well, I'm glad you like it."

"My dad tried to make it, but it was nothing like my mom's. You know, she's been dead for almost two years. She died of breast cancer."

Just the mention of his mom brought back memories for Steven. He shared with Courtney how he'd lost two important women in his life in the same year.

Feeling sad for Steven, she asked, "Who's the other woman you're referring to?"

"It was Catrina, my first love."

"Ahh, would you like some more liver pudding?" Courtney asked, quickly changing the subject. She didn't want to sadden Steven even more.

He ate two more servings and leaned over to give Courtney a big thank you kiss. She felt funny kissing him with the taste of food in her mouth, but the kiss made Courtney tingle all over and lose her senses.

Picking her up, Steven carried Courtney to the bedroom without uttering a word. Within minutes, they were in the bed naked together. Courtney moaned, longing for him to make love to her. Reading her mind, he acquiesced to her wishes.

As they lay holding each other in the aftermath of their love session, Courtney knew they would keep in touch. She felt happiness like she'd never known before. They would be distant lovers for sure.

Majesta sat up in her bed. She was in total shock. Her sisters, Kim and Jessica, had just told her that Nelson, the father of her unborn child, was a rapist.

"You're both lying," she cried, slamming down the telephone. Then she tried several times to call Courtney only to get the answering machine.

Since Majesta hated leaving messages, she kept slamming down the telephone. *I really need to talk with Courtney before I call Nelson. I need to tell her about my pregnancy.*

It had been weeks since she'd slept with Nelson. It bothered Majesta that he didn't come on to her anymore. Although she wasn't very happy about having his baby, she was trying to make the best of the situation. And she was having second thoughts about marriage.

What if he really did rape my sister? Nelson has always been a big flirt. Courtney wouldn't lie about something like that.

Majesta loved her sisters, but Courtney was her favorite before she started telling Nelson all her personal business. They were about the same dress size; Courtney just had larger breasts.

They often swapped shoes and clothes, and they both loved to dance and exercise.

She needed to hear Courtney's side of the story, so Majesta decided to call her sister again. This time, out of frustration, she left a questioning message. "Courtney, I heard something that I find hard to believe. Did Nelson rape you, sis? Please call me back so that we can talk, okay?"

Standing with the refrigerator door open, Steven overheard the message. He'd gotten hungry after their passionate love making and slipped into the kitchen for a bite to eat since Courtney was sound asleep. Steven walked over to the telephone feeling like he'd been punched in the stomach. Then he walked back to the bedroom and looked down at Courtney sleeping. He didn't know how to comfort her.

Steven climbed back into bed with Courtney and placed a gentle kiss on her forehead. He slid back into his underwear thinking about the night that he'd picked her up at the nightclub. Steven remembered how easy it had been to get her in the sack.

No matter what had happened, Steven knew that he was in love with Courtney. *That's her past. If she was raped, it wasn't her fault.*

Courtney opened her eyes to find Steven staring at her. She smile and asked, "What time is it?"

"It's nine o'clock in the morning. Your sister called, but she didn't say which one she was. She left a strange message though."

Watching Courtney sit up in bed, Steven swallowed at the sight of her full breasts. "Steven, you said I got a strange message on my answering machine."

He focused his attention on Courtney's face and replied, "Yes, some woman called and asked did some guy named Nelson rape you."

Courtney turned beet red the second the words crossed his lips. Her stomach flipped over into a knot.

Lying back down, she pulled the covers over her head. Courtney couldn't believe what she'd just heard. *Maybe it was meant for him to hear it, that way I won't have any secrets from him. Maybe this is a good time to tell him about my past.*

Before she could say anything, Steven began to speak. "Courtney, I love you, and I think we should put everything on the table right now. I'll start by telling you about my past."

Sitting up again, she tucked the sheet over her breasts, and replied, "I'm falling in love with you, too. I'm willing to share my past with you."

Hoping to break the tension between them, Steven shared some painful parts of his life. "When I was in high school, I got the crabs once from this girl that I really liked. She hurt me because I thought that I was the only one, and then I found out that she'd been with most of the guys at school. And while I've been in college, I got a girl pregnant, but she had an abortion even though I wanted the baby." He paused and swallowed before continuing.

"I admit that I wasn't ready to be a father. However, my family doesn't believe in abortion, and I was willing to make whatever sacrifices needed to be made. I still wanted a future with her, but she died that same year of heart failure. Losing her and the baby just tore me up inside. I felt like my insides had been ripped from my body, and I'd never be a whole man again. Since then, I've dated quite a bit. I just haven't found anyone that I wanted to have a lasting relationship with."

Courtney could hear the hurt in his voice and see the pain in his eyes. Feeling sorry for Steven, she wanted to hold him close.

"That's my past, and it hurts to think about it. But when I talk about it, I somehow feel better. You're the first girl that I've felt comfortable telling my story."

Giving Courtney a friendly smile, Steven looked down into her sad tear-filled eyes. He placed his hand under her chin, lifted her head, and then gave her a comforting hug.

Through tears, Courtney cried, "I was raped by my sister's boyfriend. He got me pregnant, but I got an abortion. It happened three years ago. Majesta, my sister, just found out about it. He was bragging about sleeping with me with his friends and my sister heard about it. Now I feel so ashamed that I don't know what to do."

Holding her tight, Steven felt her body trembling against his as she continued speaking, "My past hurts me, and sometimes I wish I could make that part of my life disappear. I feel that I might have led Nelson on. I found him very attractive, but it was clear that I didn't want anything to do with him sexually. He offered himself to me, and I refused. That night, he went to a club and came back drunk. The next thing I knew he was raping me. I got out my gun and almost shot him. Then a couple of weeks later, I find out that I was pregnant. I felt like I didn't have any choice but to end the pregnancy. I just couldn't bring a child into this world under those circumstances."

Courtney paused, wiping her face with her hands. "Nelson was supposed to be here to check out the campus. He thought that I wanted him because we were obviously attracted to each other. But I would never do that to my sister," she declared, staring into his eyes.

"Steven, I'm so glad all of this is out. Majesta knows and now you know, too." She went on to tell him about Alex and her office romance with, Dawson, the attorney.

"I'm not with my boss anymore. He was my last relationship, and it ended about four months ago. We're just friends," she surmised.

"I can tell from the look on your face that you're not pleased with this information, but that's my past. It's better to tell you now than to wait. I care for you dearly Steven, but I've experienced so much pain. I'm not sure if I can handle this relationship. I'll understand if you want to break up with me."

"Courtney, I'm a little shaken, but I have no right to judge you. I only worry about your leaving me to live in Texas. Do you think our relationship is strong enough to survive a long distance?"

"I think so," she replied.

"Well, I plan to keep in touch with you. I've never been in a long distance relationship before so I'll need a little time to think about it, okay?"

"Yeah, I understand."

Steven kissed Courtney, released her from his arms, and got dressed. Moments later, he quietly eased out the front door.

At the office party on Friday, Dawson presented Courtney with a gold bracelet with a charm featuring the scales of justice. She graciously accepted the gift with a gentle, "Thank you." Admitting that she still had some feelings for him she added, "I'm going to miss you."

Attorney Smith gave her a card with a one-hundred dollar bill inside. Courtney showed her appreciation by giving him a hug and a peck on the cheek. "Thanks a lot. This will go towards my moving expenses."

They had a vanilla cake with marshmallow frosting and strawberry filling custom-made for her. The party was held at one of Courtney's favorite restaurants, The Tavern.

By the time the party was over, Courtney felt exhausted and headed home to rest. Thinking back over the events of the day, she smiled inside and out.

Chapter five

Courtney started sending out invitations for her graduation the first of May. She thought about how great undergraduate school had been, but law school would be the icing on the cake. *I'm determined to do well. One day I'm going to be a successful attorney.*

Working in the law office reassured Courtney that practicing law was the career for her. Everyone in her family planned to attend the graduation, even Majesta.

They had finally talked about the rape. Courtney could tell that things had changed between her and her baby sister. Majesta decided to stay with Nelson and planned to have the baby since it was too late to have an abortion. Besides, she was in love with Nelson and wanted to find a way to forgive the father of her child. Of course, she would have to withdraw from school for a while and get a place with him.

It seemed that Courtney's sisters were drifting apart. They used to be so close before she and Majesta left Miami. Each year since they'd split up, they had a sisters' reunion. With one in Houston and two in Miami, it was becoming difficult to maintain their closeness. But Courtney didn't want to think about that right now, she had graduation and a man on her mind.

It had been a week since she'd heard from Steven. Although she'd sent him an invitation, Courtney had made up her mind not to call him.

When she finished addressing the invitations, she walked to the corner mailbox. While she was gone, Steven called and left a message on her answering machine.

"Courtney, this is Steven. It's about 3:15. Please give me a call."

Smiling, Courtney was happy to hear his voice after a week. She went into her bedroom to call Steven back. The telephone rang three times before he picked it up.

"Hello."

"Hi, Steven, it's Courtney."

"Hi, Courtney."

"I'm just returning your call. How are you doing?"

"Everything's cool."

Courtney sensed that he didn't want to talk to her so she asked, "Is something wrong?"

After a brief silence, he responded. "I really don't think that a long distance relationship will last. I just can't deal with the thought of it. So I'm going to say good-bye and wish you the best."

"But Steven—don't you want to talk about this?"

"There's nothing to discuss. Bye, Courtney." Steven hung up the telephone without giving her a chance to respond.

Courtney's stomach did a somersault. Tears slowly flowed down her face. She loved him, and felt like she'd lost her heart. Then she thought about the fact that she could be pregnant with his child. Since she missed her period this month, she planned to take a pregnancy test after graduation.

If I'm pregnant, I'm going to have the child and never tell Steven about it. I don't want him coming around just because I'm pregnant. No matter what happens, I'm going to law school.

Steven was glad that he decided to end the relationship. He simply didn't know if he could really trust Courtney. Just thinking about Nelson and the fact that she'd slept with her boss caused him much concern. He cared for her a lot but felt that he could get over her. Still, he planned on attending the graduation ceremony. Steven wanted to see Courtney just one more time. Next year, he would finish undergraduate school and move on with his life.

Attending medical school wasn't what Steven wanted even though it was exactly what his dad wanted him to do. He still had another year of undergrad before he'd have to decide.

Right now, Steven sat in bed thinking about Courtney, lusting to see her again. He knew that she would give him anything he wanted—all he had to do was say the word.

Giving in to the urge to call her, he picked up the telephone and dialed her number. "Courtney, I'm sorry. I must be crazy to think that I could just forget you. I can't stand being away from you. Please let me come over, I need to see you. I can't stand it that you're leaving the state. Please, Courtney, let me come over."

Wiping her face, Courtney cleared her voice which was still shaky from crying. "You can come over anytime you please."

Steven arrived at Courtney's apartment a little after five o'clock. Courtney answered the door wearing a tube top and biker shorts. Before he could speak, she placed a tender kiss on his lips. She'd been longing for him the whole week.

Steven returned her kiss, wrapping his arms around her waist. He felt his body changing as he closed the door, picked up Courtney, and carried her to the sofa. Looking into each other's eyes, they could see the desire they both had.

Pulling her yellow tube top over her head, Steven admired the nipples on her heavy breasts. Then Courtney pulled off her biker shorts and panties. Watching with anxious anticipation, he wished that she could be only his from this day forward.

Quickly removing his clothes, he picked Courtney up from the sofa and carried her into the bedroom. She was ready to make love right there on the sofa but was happy to be carried into her bedroom by a strong man. Thinking that she might already be pregnant, Courtney wondered if she should share her thoughts with Steven. *Would he believe me anyway?*

This time, there wasn't any gentleness during their intimacy. It didn't feel like they were making love to Courtney. Steven didn't even kiss her; he just rammed her body.

During their mating session, Courtney said, "I love you, Steven. I need you, we need you. I think I'm pregnant."

When they finished, he asked, "Courtney, why are you crying?"

"I'm going to miss you. I wish I wasn't going."

"Don't say that, honey. I'll keep in touch, maybe I'll visit you. You're going to do fine in law school."

Steven rolled over on his back, holding Courtney in his arms. Then he thought about what she'd said while their bodies were connected. *I think I'm pregnant.*

He thought she was on the pill. *I need to know if this is my child, if there is one. This is messed up. Here's a girl who I love that's moving to another state, and she might be pregnant with my baby.*

"We need to talk, Courtney, this is a serious matter. My dad could give you a pregnancy test. We'll figure out when the baby was conceived. It could very well turn out to be my baby, if you just got pregnant."

"If I'm pregnant, I know it's yours. I told you that I haven't been with anyone else but you since my last relationship ended over four months ago."

"I'm just saying… This is all happening so fast that I don't know what to think."

Courtney looked at Steven. Still crying, she felt sick. Steven wiped her face with his hands and looked straight into her eyes. He loved her so much, and if she was pregnant, he would take care of the baby.

"I know that this is the last thing you want or need right now in your life. My dad is an OB/GYN, and if you're pregnant, we can find out. Just say the word, and it's done. But you're the only one who knows whether or not you're going to keep the baby."

I'm going to keep this baby. No more abortions for me. I love Steven and I believe that he loves me, too. We'll find a way to make this work.

"Yes, Steven, I'm going to keep my baby, but I wasn't going to tell you until just now. If you hadn't come to see me, I wouldn't have told you. I don't want you to feel like you have to be there for me because you know, I'm very independent. I'm prepared to have a baby, my education is paid for, and I have money saved up."

Standing up, Courtney walked to the bathroom and started running a warm bath. Even though she wasn't planning to go anywhere, she felt compelled to bathe. After pouring bubble bath in the tub, she pulled out something sexy to wear.

Steven lay in bed with his hands behind his head, thinking about Courtney. *She is some kind of special woman. She acts like she doesn't need me. Like she has her whole life together, but I know better.*

Walking over to the bed naked, Courtney asked, "Won't you join me in the bathtub?"

Steven replied, "Sure." Although he really wanted to stay in bed and sleep, he got up, and went to the bathroom. When he got up, Courtney pulled the sheets off the bed and placed them into the dirty clothes basket.

As she entered the bathroom, Courtney turned on her radio, joining in with Keith Sweat singing "I'll Give All My Love to You." She found Steven already soaking in the tub.

Looking at him with a smile, she knew that she was in love. *He will be a good father and maybe one day a good husband.* With that thought, she slid into the tub opposite him.

They stayed in the tub talking until the bath water was cold. Getting out of the tub, she suggested, "Why don't we order a pizza and watch movies?"

He replied, "Sounds good."

Courtney had a large video collection and Steven was impressed with her variety of tastes. His favorite collection was her photographs in her picture room. She also had a horse collection. There were stuffed ones, wooden, bronze, plastic, and porcelain horses. She'd dreamed of one day having a real warm blooded black stallion of her very own.

They ate pizza and watched movies for hours. Steven hadn't planned to spend the night, but Courtney talked him into staying until her family came down for graduation.

During his stay, he made a doctor's appointment for Courtney at his dad's office. It turned out that Courtney was pregnant and possibly it was his child. It didn't matter that much to him anymore. He loved Courtney and that was the only thing that was important.

They both agreed to get a blood test done before the child was born. Although Courtney knew that she was carrying Steven's child, she wanted him to be sure of her and her love for him.

There weren't any secrets. Steven's dad knew that this could be his grandchild. He liked Courtney from the first time that he'd met her.

Dr. Palmer said, "I'm just disappointed that the baby was conceived so fast because you've only known each other for a couple of months. You two need to talk it out and do what's best for everybody." Then he added, "I'm not pleased that you're leaving the state, Courtney."

"I promise to keep in touch and to call if I have any questions about the pregnancy."

"All right, here are some pamphlets for you to review. And I want you to start taking pre-natal vitamins as well as watching your diet." He seemed concerned with her delicate condition.

"Thanks for your help, Dr. Palmer."

She and Steven walked out together holding hands, heading back to Courtney's place.

Chapter six

Being overweight can be so hard because you just don't like to shop and sometimes your face just doesn't look right. It's like you're blown out of proportion. Jessica had been the fat sister ever since her first child was born. She and Courtney both had large breasts, but Jessica had a large body to go along with hers. Although she'd lost some of the weight after the first child, she'd gained that and more back while she was pregnant with Jasmine. She simply lost control and stopped exercising.

Walking through her large closet, Jessica searched for something nice to wear to Courtney's graduation. Since she was fat, she hated buying clothes.

Standing in her closet full of clothes, shoes, and purses, she decided to put something together because she wasn't buying anymore clothes for her big butt. *My dream is to be a size nine again and then maybe William will look at me like he used to. Maybe he's seeing someone else.*

William took care of his body. Working out frequently kept him in good shape. He'd joined a local gym and invited Jessica to join him. She'd been there only once and that was over a year ago. Jessica noticed the looks that he received from all those skinny women wearing tight outfits and it bothered her. She refused to go back regardless of how many times he asked her to.

I just need to make up my mind to lose weight and keep it off, but it's so hard to do. Finally, she put together a couple of outfits and then went into Jasmine and Mariah's room to pack their clothes and toiletries. They only planned to stay a weekend in

North Carolina so they wouldn't need much. Jessica was looking forward to seeing both of her sisters.

Majesta was flying in with Nelson on Thursday. She was almost five months pregnant by now. *How will my sisters act now that everything is out in the open? I could just kill Nelson. He makes me so sick. He should stay in Houston since this is Courtney's celebration. Majesta should have made him stay, but I guess she can't trust him. She won't let him out of her sight, especially since she became pregnant.*

When Jessica finished packing, she cooked dinner and went to pick up the girls from her parents' house. William was still at work and he would go to the spa before coming home. Sometimes he didn't get home until after nine at night. *Maybe I should start going to the gym. He might not stay so late if I joined him.*

Dr. William Dean locked his doors and turned off the light in his chiropractor's office. His last patient had left over an hour ago along with the staff. He was waiting for Sandra Wells, the curvaceous woman he'd met about a month ago at The Spa, to come by. She'd said that she wanted to have sex right there in the office, so he closed the office down and sat waiting in the dark for her. He was taking a chance by giving her a key to the facility. But since her office was in the adjacent building, he figured it was okay.

Sandra arrived and pulled out the keys. William met her at the door saying, "Hello there. I've been waiting for you."

"I hope that you haven't been waiting too long. Are you ready for me?"

Without replying, William pulled her into a passionate embrace followed by a deep kiss. Before long, they were both undressed, enthralled in sexual intercourse. With Sandra on top of him, William thought, *This is something Jessica can't do anymore because of her weight. Oh, how I wish she'd lose some of those pounds.*

After minutes of rolling, humping, and kissing all over the office floor, they were exhausted. "That was worth the wait."

"Why thank you, William. I aim to please."

"Hmm, thanks for pleasing me."

"I have to get dressed and get home to my husband. Maybe we can do this again sometime," she replied, fixing her bra.

William got dressed and went to the spa. There he showered, worked out for awhile, and headed home. Dinner was on the stove waiting for him. William saw Jessie's packed bags by the door.

Knowing that he really didn't want to go on the trip, he gently closed the front door. Standing there, he could hear the television on in the bedroom.

The girls were sleeping. Jessie sat up eating a bag of Lay's potato chips with a diet soda on a tray beside the bed. She always had a midnight snack before going to bed. Dinner was never enough for her. She didn't get much exercise except for eating. She would eat a huge lunch everyday and then come home and cook a large dinner.

Today she had cooked fried fish with sweet peas, mashed potatoes, and honey buttered rolls. She and her family loved seafood. That's all they ate when she was a child. Her father would bring some type of seafood home almost every evening. And Jessie's children didn't care much for burgers and fries like most kids. But sometimes she'd order them a pizza.

William didn't allow Jasmine and Mariah to eat junk food. He wanted them to eat healthy meals everyday. They couldn't eat any candy, only fruit or fruit snacks and yogurt instead of ice cream.

William walked into the bedroom to find Jessie eating at a late hour again. "Hi," he said, staring at the bag in her hand. Then he headed to the bathroom to take another shower.

"Hey," she responded, putting the chips down.

Jessie rolled out of bed. It was getting harder each day for her to move normally. Her weight was about 200 pounds and she stood at only five feet four inches tall. She just couldn't get enough when she was on her period. That's when she ate the most.

William couldn't stand to look at his wife. He was a handsome fair skinned man carrying 190 pounds on his six foot two inch frame. Certainly, he was a good father and a great provider for his family. It was tearing him apart to see Jessica eat like she did. He'd tried to get her to go to the spa with him as well as get on an exercise program, but she refused.

"William, can I come in honey?" she asked, cracking the bathroom door.

"Yes, Jessie."

"How was your day? I started to come by the office, but mama called. You know, I couldn't get her off the telephone. Dad is upset about Majesta taking Nelson to the graduation. He said if he could, he would kill Nelson. It hurts him and mama that we had to keep the whole thing a secret for so long. But I told them that Courtney really didn't want them to know. Besides, Majesta is a bitch now. She said that she doesn't blame Courtney, but I think that she does. You know, Daddy never liked Nelson much anyway. Now he can't stand to even see him. He also told mama that Nelson can't set foot in his house ever again. Mama just went on and on about it. I just hope there will not be any problems."

Listening in silence, William turned the shower on and entered the stall. He really didn't care about a thing Jessica was talking about. *I just wish she'd shut up and go to bed.*

Noticing how disinterested he seemed, Jessica walked out, gently closing the door behind her. She put the bag of chips in the kitchen and threw the soda can in the garbage. With tears flowing down her cheek, her heart was breaking into pieces. *I see the disgust in his eyes when he looks at me. He doesn't even listen to me anymore. He just stays away as much as possible.*

Jessica hated their king size bed because Williams slept all the way on the other side. He was so close to the edge on most nights, she was afraid that he'd fall out of the bed if she turned over.

I wonder if he's going to North Carolina with me and the girls. I don't want to force him so I'll just wait and see what he says when he comes out of the bathroom.

Kimberly had packed her family's things for the trip. They'd planned to leave at two o'clock the next morning. She talked to her parents, Courtney, and Majesta.

Knowing that she needed to talk to Jessica, she picked up the telephone and dialed the number. "Hello?"

"Hello, sis, what's up?

"I was just getting ready to go to bed. Are you ready for the drive to North Carolina?" Jessie asked.

"Yes, we're all ready to go. The boys couldn't half sleep because they're so excited."

"The girls and I are packed, but William doesn't act as if he wants to go. He's been acting funny lately. I think he's messing around on me. Maybe it would be better for the both of us if he would stay home. Maybe we should separate. I can tell he doesn't want me, Kim. We haven't kissed or hugged in weeks. I told you the last time we had sex was more than two months ago and he still seems disinterested. That hurts me so much. I feel like nothing. I look like a fat pig. I really don't feel like going anywhere, but I need to be around my sisters. Maybe Courtney has a good diet plan for me. You know she's going to get on me about my weight."

"Girl, you need to tell him how you're hurting, and ya'll need to talk. If you believe there is another woman, tell him, and you really need to lose weight. It's not healthy for you, sis, to be so big. I remember when you wore a size nine, couldn't keep you out of the beauty shop, and we walked all the time."

"Well, I'm not the size that I want to be, but I'm comfortable."

"Don't worry about that grown man. You and the girls are flying so you don't have to depend on him to drive. If he doesn't use the ticket, maybe you can get the money back."

"You might be right."

"Anyway, I'm looking forward to this reunion with my sisters. I'm going to be there with bells on. It's always fun when we get together."

"Alright, I'll see you soon," Jessie replied, hanging up the telephone. Entering the bedroom, she found her husband asleep. Jessie turned on the lights to wake him up because she was ready to talk. William opened his eyes slightly, and then closed them again. He thought Jessica was getting something off the nightstand.

Sitting on the side of the bed, Jessie looked at her polished toes. "William, wake up. We need to talk."

William turned over, looking at his wife as she sat on the bed wearing a house dress. No matter how fat she was, Jessie was still pretty. Her hair was long and she wore it parted down the center with two braids on each side at night. She kept herself and her home well cleaned. Once upon a time, she had a nice shape but when that all changed, William lost his attraction to her.

"Are you going with me and the girls to North Carolina?"

"I don't think I need to go, Jessie. I got too much work at the office and besides, I don't want to go," he abruptly replied, showing his irritation with her question. As far as he was concerned, this marriage was over and he didn't see any reason to be cordial to his wife or her family.

"Ok then, I'll just try to get the money back for your ticket. And in the future, I will not include you in the family vacations. The girls and I are going to do our thing. And while I got your attention, what in the hell is your problem? You act like the sun rises and sets on your black ass. You act as if there's someone else. Maybe now you and whoever that home wrecker is can spend some time together," Jessie replied, expressing her bitterness. Something inside was telling her that he had another woman whether he was willing to admit it not. She was going with her intuitions.

Looking at Jessica, William sat up in bed. Everything she'd said was right on target, but he wasn't going to agree. He knew that she would leave with the girls. And since he loved his babies, he couldn't take the chance.

"Listen, Jessie, I'm tired, and I don't like to argue. I need to get some sleep for tomorrow. I don't care what I act like. I just don't find you attractive anymore. I told you how I feel about fat women so don't act like you're so surprised. I'm going to bed now, and I would appreciate it if you would turn the lights off, and go sleep somewhere else."

"Whatever. I don't want to sleep with you no way. I like the bed in the other room," Jessie huffed. Walking away from him, she switched off the light, and went to sleep in the guest room. Jessie was determined not to let him see how hurt she was from his words and used the time alone to cry a sea of tears.

At four o'clock the next morning, Mariah went to the bathroom then to her parents' room to sleep in their bed. Jessica left the light on in the bathroom for their three and a half year old daughter. Most of the time when Mariah didn't go back to her bed, she'd join her parents' in their king sized bed. This time, she found her mama missing. Shaking her daddy, she said, "Wake up."

"What—what is it baby girl?"

"Daddy, where's mommy?"

"She's in the other room. Climb on in here with daddy."

Snuggling close to her Dad, Mariah went back to sleep while William stared at the space where his wife normally was.

Jessica woke up early Wednesday morning with Kim and her family on her mind. *They must be on the road to North Carolina by now. I can't wait for Friday to come. I'm ready to get away from William for a while.*

She cleaned up; making sure that the girls had everything for the trip. Tomorrow, she planned to get her hair and nails done at her sister's shop. Since Kim had hired Da'won, things had been going pretty well. He could do some hair, too. And Jessica would let only him do her hair style when Kim couldn't do it. Kim wouldn't have left so early in the week either if Da'won wasn't there helping out.

By seven that morning, she was finished with her cleaning. Jasmine, her nine-month-old was ready to eat. Every morning she stood up in her crib calling her mama, but sometimes she would call daddy, too. Mariah and Jasmine both had pretty hair. Mariah was yellow and skinny. Jasmine had caramel skin. Jasmine loved to eat, but Mariah didn't care if she ate or not.

Jessica prepared the girls cream of wheat with toast. She got Mariah's vitamins out of the cabinet and poured her apple juice in a cup. Jasmine had a bottle until her food cooled off.

There she was, standing in her crib waiting. Jessica picked her up, kissed her, and then changed her diaper. She gave the baby a bottle and laid her back in the crib. Jessica went back in the kitchen to make some coffee and read the newspaper. William was still asleep, but she placed a cup of coffee on the table for him. He didn't normally eat breakfast like she and the girls did.

Jessica wanted to work so badly, but she had stopped when she and William got married. They'd been married for five years and she was tired of being at home. She asked William if she could work in his office lots of times, but William said, "A husband and wife shouldn't work together."

Since she loved taking care of children, Jessica planned to go back to school and get her degree so that she could open a daycare facility. But William didn't want his children in a daycare right now. Jessie's mother told her she would love to watch her grandchildren while Jessie went to college. The children loved their Granny Dee.

Jessica got her weight problem from dear old mom because she loved to eat, too. She always visits the food court in the mall whenever she's shopping. Jessica and her mother often went to the grocery store to get whatever they were craving. It seemed like they craved a different pastry each week. They lived within walking distance of the mall, and even now Courtney gets excited when she visits Miami. She usually goes to the mall and sees her high school friends who work there.

I hope that William doesn't mind my mom watching the girls. Diane was a nurse who kept a clean home, and she loved her grandchildren. William's parents lived in Georgia and the girls really didn't know them. Jessica felt that it might have bothered him a little.

Jessica decided to call her mom. "Hi there, is there anything you need me to pick up for you and dad?"

"No, sweetie, we're fine. We'll see you tomorrow when you pick us up."

"Okay, Courtney is going to meet us at the airport. So everything is set."

"All right then. You know, Majesta and Nelson are leaving on Thursday from Houston. They'll catch a cab to their hotel from the airport."

"Yeah, it's best that they don't go to Courtney's house without us. How're they doing anyway?"

"They seem to be getting along pretty well. Even though I don't see how she stays with that tramp, baby or no baby. I wouldn't have him."

"Me, neither, Mom."

"Anyway, I don't want to waste my breathe talking about that fool. It'll just run up my blood pressure."

"Okay, try to get some rest. I'll see you all around five o'clock tomorrow evening then."

After William kissed the girls good bye and left for work, Jessie took them to visit the fish market. She bought some fried conch and fried fish for the girls. *I don't care if William eats anything. It's obvious that he has another woman in his life. So he can cook for himself this weekend. I plan to clean the house and make sure that there is clean laundry, but as for planning his meals, no way.*

Once they left the fish market, Jessie went to the dollar store in the mall to buy some black rubber bands and hair bows for the girls' hair. She also let Mariah pick out a toy or two for herself and her sister. Jessie loved the dollar store just as much as they did.

When they arrived home, she and Mariah ate the dinner consisting of fried conch meat, homemade French fries with the skin, a roll, couch sauce, and a lime. Jasmine ate two jars of her favorite baby food, and then Jessica gave her a bottle and put her down for a nap. Mariah watched television until she fell asleep.

Jessica watched all of her favorite soap operas while the girls slept. She'd already cleaned the house and finished packing for the trip. Jessica thought about William as she watched one of the stories. *Lately, William hasn't shown me any affection. We've only been married for five years, and he's already tired of me. Why can't we be happy like Kim and Carlton? They seem so happy.*

Carlton had tried to get William to double date, but William never had the time. Jessica had to beg her husband to go to family gatherings. She was tired of trying to make him happy. He just didn't care anymore. *I love him dearly but I have to give him some space. I know he's having sex with someone else so I'm not going to sleep with him even if he wants me to. He needs to have an AIDS test before he touches me again.*

Around seven o'clock, she made some grits and dinner rolls. The fish was boiled with lemon juice, garlic salt, red and yellow bell peppers, onions, and some Miami seafood seasoning.

This was a light non-fat dish. Jessica loved fish and grits and so did William, but he would probably get home too late to eat dinner. *Hopefully, he'll get home early enough on Friday to take us to the airport.*

Jessica cleaned the kitchen and put the dishes away after eating her dinner. Then, she fell asleep in the guest bedroom.

As William entered the door, he smelled the food. He headed for the kitchen and fixed himself a hefty portion. William ate the food while watching an episode of *Miami Vice*. Then he washed the bowl out and took a shower.

After his shower, he went into the girls' room and kissed Mariah. Jasmine woke up when he entered the bedroom, so he picked her up and took her into the Florida room to watch some television. *I'll miss my babies if anything happens between Jessie and me.*

He'd planned to take the girls to see his parents this summer. *Jessica will probably want to go, but I'm not interested in taking her anywhere with me, especially to my parents home. They never liked her anyway. Maybe she'll welcome a break from the girls.*

Jasmine looked at her daddy and kissed him on the cheek. "Eat, eat, daddy," she begged.

William got up and gave her a baby cookie for teething. He fixed her a bottle of milk. She went right back to sleep.

Kissing her on the forehead, he took her back to bed passing the guest room where Jessie was sleeping. *I hope she sleeps in there from now on. I can't stand the sight of her.*

Jessie woke up around 1:30 that morning longing to be in her husband's arms. She wished that she could get into her own bed with William making sweet love to her. Jessica couldn't get back to sleep because she was excited from just thinking about her husband. She wanted him right then, but she knew he wouldn't have her, so Jessie laid in the bed thinking, *Maybe he just needs some space for awhile. I'll stay in the guest room until we can work things out.*

Thursday morning, Jessie woke up with swollen red eyes from crying herself to sleep. This rejection was killing her. She didn't even have an appetite for anything this morning.

William woke up early so that he was gone when the girls got out of the bed. Jessie called his office to see if he was there. It was 7:30 when William answered the telephone. The staff hadn't arrived yet since the office didn't open until 9:00 a.m.

"William Dean, Chiropractor's office."

"Good morning, Dr. Dean, this is your wife. I'm sorry we've been missing each other these days. It doesn't take a rocket scientist to realize that you don't give a damn about me. I want you to know that I love you dearly, but if you need some space, it's yours. I'll sleep in the guest bedroom as long as you want me to. Just remember that I'm still your wife so a simple 'Hi' or 'Bye' would do."

"Jessie, what are you talking about?"

"The girls and I plan to spend the summer in Houston with Courtney. I'm going to make arrangements while I'm down there on this trip. I know that you love the girls, but I'm not leaving them. I'm their only caregiver anyway. I plan to stay at least one month in Houston. I'm tired of staying at home waiting for my husband who doesn't care if I live or die. I have feelings, William, and right now I'm depressed. You need to decide what you want."

William listened to his wife who was crying by now, talking in a very low voice. He could tell that she was hurting, but he didn't care. "The only thing that's bothering me is that you're taking the girls for a whole month. This'll be the first time that we've been separated that long."

"I know that."

"But I have to go to work, and I can't think of anyone they could stay with except for you or your parents. They don't really know my parents. Maybe they can go visit them when you all get back. My parents want to see them, too."

"I don't know, we'll have to talk about that."

"Jessica, I'm sorry. Right now, I don't feel love for you," he said, pausing for a second.

"Maybe we should think about getting a divorce. I love my girls, and I hope you will not try to take them from me. We can work something out regarding visitation. I know a good lawyer who works in my building. I've been talking to him and he needs to talk to you, because I just want to be free. If you're planning to stay in Houston for a month, I think that's too long. How would you feel if I left for a month and took the girls?"

Jessica remained silent. Then she screamed through her tears, "I wouldn't trust you to take my babies anywhere for one day."

"I'm a good father. What do you mean by that?"

"William, you don't do much for them daily. You don't even know what foods they like to eat. Besides, I know what you're all about. You're probably planning to take that home wrecker with you," she said, feeling the anger rising from the pit of her stomach. "Well, I don't think so Mr. Dean. And one more thing before I put Mr. Click on the phone, I don't need to talk to your damn attorney. I'll be glad to get that divorce as soon as possible. You make me sick, and I hope that you catch something, you dirty dog. And don't worry about taking us to the airport, we'll catch a cab."

Jessica slammed the telephone down and sat at the kitchen table madder than the time when she kicked Tracey Nickerson's butt back in high school. If William had been at home, she would have kicked his butt, too. She decided at that moment that she wouldn't cry anymore for William Dean. Jessie made some coffee, fed Mariah and Jasmine, and left to spend the day at her parents.

Chapter seven

Arriving at her mother's house, Jessica turned on the television set for Mariah and Jasmine to watch *Sesame Street*. Her dad was still in the bed, but her mother was in the kitchen preparing breakfast. Jessica had her own key so her mother didn't hear her come in. She didn't call out so her mom wasn't expecting her. When Diane turned to see her daughter walking in, she knew something was wrong. With puffy eyes, Jessie looked sad and angry.

Diane gave her daughter a hug and said, "Sit down. Try to eat some breakfast."

"No, mom, I'm not hungry," she replied, still standing, hanging her head. Diane could see the tears drop from Jessie's eyes. Something was seriously wrong because her eating partner wasn't eating.

"What's wrong, baby, why are you crying?" she asked, pulling out a chair. "Sit down and tell mama what's going on."

Taking a seat next to her mother, Jessie spoke, "Mama, William doesn't love me anymore. He wants a divorce. I told him that I'd give him one because I can't live with a man that doesn't love me. He looks at me like—I'm crap. He thinks I'm too fat, so if he only wants me when I'm slim and pretty, I don't need him anyway. It's been hard to take this weight off. I know I got some bad eating habits, but I'm going to do something about it. I plan to visit Courtney this summer for a month so that I can lose some weight and at the same time, I would be giving William some space. I planned that before he asked me for a divorce."

Placing an arm around her daughter's shoulder, Diane stated, "I'm sorry that you're going through this, baby. But it's better for you to be alone than to be unhappy with him. Your children don't need to see you looking like this. Are you going to be all right until tomorrow night?"

"Yes, mama. The girls and I are going to take a cab to the airport. We'll be gone before he comes home. Besides, I've been sleeping in the guest bedroom since last week. Kim told me to do that and leave him alone for awhile. Mama, I know he's sleeping around, and if I catch him he wouldn't get visiting rights with the children. I don't want some other woman around my babies."

"Sweetheart, think about what you're saying."

"He asked if he could take them to see his parents in Georgia. I told him no. I'm sure the other woman is going because William doesn't care for me so he doesn't care about my feelings. I can't wait to get away, and I'm thinking about staying longer than one weekend. I'm going to go home and pack some more things. I'm sure we wouldn't be missed by Dr. Dean."

"Jessie, be careful and go slow because a divorce can be hard on you. You know how much he loves those girls. If he can dig something up on you, he will. I don't trust that scoundrel."

"I know. When I get back, I'm going to talk to an attorney. I have to protect myself and my children. I don't know what he's going to try on me," Jessie replied, wiping the last of her tears away. *It's time to start pulling myself together,* she thought.

About ten o'clock that morning, Mr. Charles woke up to the smell of breakfast cooking. Jessica helped him into his wheelchair and rolled him into the kitchen where Mariah was waiting. When Mariah saw her granddaddy, she ran and kissed his hands. While watching his grandbaby, Mrs. Charles put his plate of buttered grits, toast, turkey bacon, and poached eggs on the T.V. tray.

Taking a piece of bacon, Mariah sat down on the kitchen floor. Jessica and her mother joined the two of them, but told Mariah, "You can go watch television in your grandparents' bedroom when you finish eating your bacon."

"All right, mommy."

As soon as Mariah left the room, Jessica pulled up a chair and started telling her daddy all about her marital problems. Looking at his daughter with sad eyes, he replied, "Daddy won't let William hurt his baby." He felt so helpless sometimes because of his disability, but he wouldn't let anyone harm his family. And Jessica was the closest daughter to him. She told her daddy things that she hadn't even told her mother.

    Jessica kissed her daddy's hand, and then gave him a big hug. They sat and watched television as they talked for several minutes.

    Diane called Jessica into her bedroom so that she could help her check their luggage. They checked for Mr. Charles's medication and his toiletries. "Well, mama, it looks like you have everything packed."

    "I think so, baby. Let's take all these suitcases into the living room and clean up a little."

    Later, they prepared some sandwiches with vinegar chips and tea cakes. Jessica made some iced tea and gave the girls some apple juice. When they were finished eating, her parents, Mariah, and Jasmine took a nap while Jessica stayed up watching television.

    That afternoon, Jessie called and cancelled her appointment at Kim's salon. She didn't feel like going anymore. William had upset her to the point that all she wanted to do was stay with her parents until she took them to the airport.

    A few hours later, Jessica drove her parents to the airport. Their first class flight departed at seven o'clock. After checking in their luggage, she went as far as she could with them in the terminal. She and the girls kissed them and gave them good-bye hugs. Then Jessica watched her mother push her father down the terminal way until they were out of sight.

By the time she and the girls got home, it was almost nine o'clock. They'd gotten on the turnpike, making it back right at the girls bedtime.

    When she walked in the house, she was surprised to see William sitting in the Florida room watching television. He was eating some leftovers; and the bowl of fish and grits was still in his hand. A half-empty bottle of Coke was sitting on the table.

Looking at him, she went to lay Jasmine in her crib. Mariah went to her daddy to get some of his dinner. He fed her some, and then went to heat up some more for himself.

Jessica stomped to the bathroom and started running a bath for Mariah. She was still too angry to even speak to her husband. Just as she put Mariah to bed, Jasmine woke up. William gave her some baby food and walked around with her for a few minutes.

Jessica took a quick shower, put on her gown, and headed to the Florida room. She picked up Jasmine, who was on the floor with her toys, and gave her a bath, too. Jessie let Jasmine stay in the guest bedroom with her until she fell asleep.

When Jessie put Jasmine in the crib, she could see that William was still up. Looking at him, she said, "Good night."

He threw up his hand in response, but didn't say a word. So Jessie got in the bed and went on to sleep.

William was in the shower when Jessie woke up. He was leaving early again. Moments later, he slipped out of the house without speaking to her, but he kissed the girls and told Mariah, "I'll see you when you get back."

What William doesn't know won't hurt him. He probably wouldn't miss us anyway. Let him wonder. And if he doesn't know when we're coming back, I can surprise him and the other woman.

Jessie cleaned up before the girls woke up. She made sure that everything was packed and added more things for the additional week they would be staying.

While cleaning, Jessie found an envelope on the dresser with her name on it. It was money for the trip. One thing about William, he was free hearted. She was sure that the other woman was getting her share of their money, too.

After placing the money in her purse, Jessie changed all the sheets on the beds, disinfected all the bathrooms, mopped the floors, and vacuumed the carpet. She still needed to wash some clothes, but it was almost time for the girls to wake up so she made cream of wheat with raisins and a cup of coffee for herself.

William had changed, and Jessica wondered what kind of affect this woman had on him. She made up her mind to check out things when she got back, to find out about the woman that stole her man.

At noon, she and the girls sat down to watch television. After a couple of hours, she gave the girls a bath, took one herself, and laid out their clothes. The girls were dressed alike in red, white, and blue sailor outfits with black shoes. Jessie dressed in jeans and a red blouse. She and her sister, Kim, always dressed like their children or coordinated the colors with what they wore. If they wore black and white, so did the children.

At five o' clock, they dressed and called the cab to take them to the airport. A Cuban gentleman pulled up in the driveway. Jessica had the luggage on the front porch. She really didn't like the fact that they had to drive around with a stranger.

Making sure that she had her sharp silver nail file in her purse, they watched the driver load the cab, and climbed into the back seat. He took the turnpike which was the quickest way to the airport. If he'd gone another way, she would have told him to turn around.

They boarded the airplane headed to North Carolina that evening at 7:08. Courtney, Kim, and hopefully, Majesta, would meet them at the air terminal.

Jasmine slept the whole trip and was still asleep when the airplane landed. However, Mariah talked the whole way. "Mama, is the plane in the sky? Do you think it would crash like the one we saw on TV? Mama, I'm scared. Mama, can you tell that man who's driving us to stop so we can get off? Mama, when are we going to get there?" She went on and on until Jessie gave her a coloring book and crayons that she'd remembered to pack in her carry-on bag.

Jessica was so relieved that the trip was over. When the airplane landed, they were the first ones to exit. "Bye-bye," she said, waving at the airline stewardesses. *Thank God for a safe flight.*

Once they were out of the tunnel, Jessie felt someone grab her. It was Courtney. They hadn't seen each other in over a year. Courtney took her bag and before she knew it, Majesta was hugging her, too. Then Kim hugged Jessie and said, "I'm glad you had a safe trip."

"Me, too. I'm not very fond of flying."

Jessica cried, kissed, and embraced her sisters in a group hug. *They look so pretty. I really need to lose weight. I look like a whale beside them.*

Mariah looked at the two aunts that she didn't know. She walked up to Aunt Kim and took her by the hand.

Although Majesta was pregnant, she was still skinny. She had on maternity clothes, but she wasn't showing much. Courtney looked great like always. She had on some jeans and a pink blouse and sandals to match.

All of the sisters went to Courtney's place where their parents, and Kim's husband and children were waiting. Kim and Majesta had made reservations at a local hotel about fifteen minutes away.

Courtney had a room for her parents to sleep in. Jessica and the girls would stay with her and sleep on the sofa bed. Courtney said it was all right for them to stay a week at her place. Their parents were only staying for the weekend. The sisters were happy to be together again. They sat in the living room talking about everything from Jessica's weight to Courtney's new guy. Nelson wasn't mentioned once. Majesta left him at the hotel, and he had planned to go clubbing.

Jessica told her sisters about how William was treating her and how she was going to lose some weight. Courtney told her sisters about Steven and her pregnancy. Majesta was almost five months pregnant and still having morning sickness. She finally had breasts that were noticeable. "I'm really excited about having a baby," she beamed.

Yeah, but the father is a creep. Courtney couldn't fight the thoughts running through her mind. She'd felt that maybe the pregnancies might make she and her sister close again. *But there's still distance between us. I can feel it.*

Kim and Jessica talked about their pregnancies and the painful deliveries they'd had. Kim said, "My twins were so small that I hated leaving them in the hospital for two months. They each weighed only two pounds."

The other sisters looked at the twins, Drake and Blake, as they played with Mariah and Jasmine. "You'd never think that they'd been such small babies," Jessica commented.

Jeremy played with his race cars while Carlton, Jr., sat at the table with his daddy eating a burger with fries. Kim started humming "Hold On" by En Vogue, and her sisters joined in with her in harmony for a minute since it was one of their favorite songs, too.

It was getting late and they had to get up early so Majesta, Kim, and Kim's family drove back to the hotel. Majesta had told Nelson that she would get a ride to the hotel so that he didn't have to pick her up.

Once they were gone, Courtney helped her mother put Mr. Charles to bed. Jessica got the sofa bed ready for Mariah and herself. Jasmine was sleeping with her grandparents.

Before long, Courtney's guests were asleep. She called Steven to see what he was doing. "Hello," he answered, sounding tired.

"Steven, did I wake you? I was just calling to see if you were coming to the ceremony?"

"Yes, you know I am."

"It starts at 11:00 a.m. so be there at ten so that you can sit with my family. We plan to go to a restaurant after graduation. Can you come?"

"Yes, sweetheart, but you better let me get some sleep so that I can get up."

"Good night, baby, I'll see you in the morning."

Courtney hung up the telephone and tidied up her place. She washed the dishes and wiped off everything. Then she checked the locks on the windows and doors several times. At least she could take a bath and go to bed knowing that Kim would come by early to do her hair and nails. She was planning to wear a black and white dress.

Courtney woke up at 6:00 on Saturday morning completely excited. But she was beginning to feel her pregnancy. She felt like throwing up. Instead she went to the refrigerator for some apple juice. That didn't do any good.

After she threw up, she felt a little better. She chewed some gum to overcome the taste in her mouth. It was 7:15 when she heard Jasmine wake up.

Knocking on the door, she entered the room where her parents were sleeping. Jasmine sat up in the bed between her grandparents looking around at the unfamiliar place. Diane sat up and started talking to the baby.

Courtney said, "Good morning." She reached for Jasmine, but the baby turned away. Since she was only nine months old, she didn't know her Aunt Courtney and Aunt Majesta very well. They'd only seen her twice since her birth.

"Go to Aunt Courtney, Jazzie Poo. Give Aunt Courtney a big hug and kiss."

Jasmine shook her little head with a smile and lay on the bed with her feet in her hands. She was a beautiful baby with soft curly hair. Courtney wanted a baby just like her.

"I think we should eat at the Pancake House next to the hotel where Kim and Majesta are staying."

"Okay, I'll start getting your dad ready so we won't make you late. Are you excited, baby?"

"Yes, mama, I am. I guess working at a law firm helped the time fly by."

Courtney picked up Jasmine in spite of her crying. Giving the baby a hug and a kiss on the neck, she took the yelling child to her mother who was asleep on the sofa bed.

When Jessica heard Jasmine crying, she woke up. Courtney put the baby in the bed with her mother. "Mama needs to change that baby."

Jessica got up and took a Pamper and wipes out of the baby bag. Courtney watched her sister while she changed Jasmine. She couldn't wait until she could be a mother.

Jessica kissed her baby and laid her down next to Mariah, who was still asleep. She and Courtney walked to the kitchen. Jessica fixed Jasmine a bottle and gave it to her. Courtney sat at the kitchen table and called Kim.

"Hello, Kim, speaking."

"Kim, let's meet at the Pancake House next to the hotel for breakfast. Mama is getting daddy ready so we could probably be there by nine."

"Okay, sis, we're all pretty hungry. I was getting ready to call room service for breakfast, but nine is fine. We'll see ya'll there."

"Okay, tell Majesta to get ready and meet us there. I hope she doesn't bring Nelson."

"She's mad at him, anyway. He went to a club last night and stayed out really late. She was calling him all kinds of names this morning."

"She doesn't need to be getting upset. I can't understand why she brought him anyway. She is getting so damn silly. You can't tell her nothing about that no good man. He's a low down dirty dog. Majesta needs to wake up and smell the coffee. I know he's messing around. He's just the type who could catch AIDS. If I was Majesta, I wouldn't sleep with him. Girl, let me get off this telephone and get dressed. Don't worry about my hair, we won't have anytime anyway. See you later, sis."

As soon as Courtney was off the telephone with Kim, she called Steven. "Hi, can you meet us for breakfast?"

"Sure, just tell me where, and I'm there."

Courtney gave him the details and said, "You can leave your car at the restaurant and ride with us in the custom van that I rented for the weekend."

"Cool, see you shortly."

Courtney took a shower and brushed her hair up into a ponytail. She laid her black and white dress on her bed and took out some matching pumps.

When she was through making up her face, she put on a coat of cotton candy nail polish. As she sat blowing her nails dry, she began thinking about Steven. She thought about their unborn child, picturing herself holding a baby in her arms. However, her happy thoughts soon turned to sad ones. *Steven will be staying in North Carolina while I'm in Texas. I'll be going though my pregnancy alone. Steven promised to visit me twice a month on the weekends but that's not good enough. At least Majesta has that no good Nelson around her all the time.*

Courtney was beginning to feel miserable and depressed especially with the morning sickness. She wanted her man around to hold her when she was sick and when the baby started moving, he could place his hands on her stomach. It would be nice to have him go with her to check-ups. *Will he be there when the baby is born?* She wondered.

Abortion never entered Courtney's mind because she wanted this baby more than anything. Courtney felt a tremble come over her. The tears welled up in her eyes, her ears and neck felt hot. She didn't feel like she could get through the day.

Closing her door, she locked it. Then she moved her clothes to a chair and got in bed. She cried until her anxiety attack was over. If she didn't cry, it would build up until she cracked later in the day. *There must be someway we can be together. Maybe I should delay law school.*

Moments later, Courtney got up and realized that she'd messed up her nails. She got out the nail remover and put on a new coat of nail polish. Then she got herself together and went into the living room with Jessica and the girls. Jessica was combing Mariah's hair while Jasmine, who had already been fed and dressed, lay asleep on the sofa. She put Mariah's hair in four ponytails with yellow and white bows to match her dress. Mariah's dress lay on the sofa next to Jasmine.

"What have you been doing, Courtney? Are you feeling all right, sis?"

"I'm okay; I just wish Steven was going to Texas with me. I want him to be with me. Here I am pregnant and the father won't be there with me. It takes something away from the joy of being pregnant. I want to go to sleep with him at night and wake up by his side. Every time I think about our separation, it makes me so sad, Jessie."

Courtney felt the tears well up in her eyes again. She should be happy, but she wasn't. Could she get through this day?

"Sis, it's going to be all right. Just take one day at a time and enjoy this day. We are so proud of you and if you and Steven love each other, everything will work out. If it's God's will for you to be together, you will. Don't worry about tomorrow; just be glad that you are alive today. Stop crying and go to your room and fix your make-up. It was so pretty."

Courtney smiled and gave her sister a kiss on the cheek. "I don't know what I'd do without you," she whispered.

"That's what sister's are for. Now go."

By 8:45 a.m., everyone was dressed. Courtney got the keys to the van, loaded up everybody, and headed for the Pancake House. When they arrived, Kim and her family were walking in the door. Courtney didn't see Majesta and wondered if she was waiting inside.

She parked the van and waited for everyone to go inside. Steven sat on a bench waiting for her; Kim and her family stood close by. Courtney smiled at how close they were standing next to Steven. Now she could introduce everyone.

Looking around for Majesta, Courtney realized that she wasn't there. They walked over to Kim's family, then Courtney walked a few steps to Steven and grabbed his arm. "Steven, this is my family."

Steven looked at the beautiful people in front of him and said, "Hello, everybody. It's a pleasure to meet you all." He'd already noticed Kim. She was pretty just like Courtney. He looked at the pretty woman standing behind the curly haired man in a wheelchair and thought that they made a lovely couple.

Kim and Jessica looked at Steven with wide eyes and Colgate smiles. Courtney introduced them by name and told him that her baby sister hadn't made it there yet. Courtney whispered in Kim's ear, "Where's Majesta?"

Kim looked at her strangely. She was keeping something from Courtney. "Well, let's just sit down and eat something. We're all hungry," Kim said.

They sat in the non-smoking area. After the waitress took their orders, it took about fifteen minutes to bring their food out. As the waitress was placing the food on the table, Majesta walked in with Nelson by her side. Courtney felt betrayed. The frustration she felt was unbearable.

Feeling like all eyes were on her, Courtney held her breath. Steven held her hand, looking into her eyes. He looked at the dark-skinned girl who favored Courtney and knew that had to be the rapist with her. Steven looked around at the family. They all had disgust written on their faces. *How could Majesta do this to her sister? Didn't she believe Courtney?*

Steven felt like punching Nelson's lights out. Majesta, now five months pregnant, slowly walked to the table looking like she was feeling sick. She wore a purple and gold silk maternity pants set. Nelson walked behind her acting like he was shy. "Good morning. How y'all doing?" Majesta inquired. Nelson simply waved a hand and mumbled, "Good morning." Everyone turned away or pretended to be eating their food.

Courtney felt her ears turn beet red which always happened when she was upset, excited, or mad. Majesta and Nelson sat at a booth next to them. Majesta looked over at Steven and smiled. *He's gorgeous.*

Sensing the anger that the family had for him, Nelson knew that he'd done Courtney wrong. *But she did lead me on, she asked for it. I couldn't control myself because I was drunk. Well, they can all kiss my butt, even the guy with Courtney who keeps looking at me.*

Everyone, except Majesta and Nelson, was finished eating and sat around talking for a while. Mr. Charles really liked Steven; he thought that the young man had a good head on his shoulders. He was ashamed that two of his daughters were pregnant and not married. *I wish they weren't pregnant. That Nelson is no good. I knew that right away.*

Majesta had changed so much since he last saw her. She seemed different somehow, and it was hard to talk to her. College and Nelson had changed his baby girl a lot.

Courtney only ate some fruit and toast. She really didn't have an appetite these days. All she wanted was grape juice or apple juice. Steven touched her stomach and said, "You need to eat so that you and the baby will get proper nourishment."

Placing her hand on top of his, she simply smiled at him. Courtney loved the attention he was giving her. She would miss him when they went their separate ways.

Courtney asked Carlton, "Can you drive the van? It's too large for me. I felt like I was driving a school bus on the way over here. I just rented it to accommodate the family."

Carlton nodded his head, took the keys, and got into the van. Steven parked his car closer to the hotel and jumped into the van with all of them.

Majesta and Nelson finished their meal and hurried to catch up with the family. She huffed, "They didn't have to leave us like that. They barely spoke to us the whole time, anyway. What's up with them?"

Nelson said, "It's okay. I remember where the campus is, we don't have to rush."

Courtney graduated with high honors, bringing tears of joy to the eyes of her family. When Courtney Marie Charles' name was called, she could hear their screams loud and clear. She smiled, blowing kisses to them as she received her degree.

Majesta and Nelson were late because Nelson got lost. They missed Courtney receiving her degree. The family didn't see Majesta and Nelson at the ceremony because they were way in the back. After the ceremony was over, the family went to a cafeteria because everyone had a taste for different things.

However, Majesta and Nelson got a bite to eat at a local fast food restaurant and headed back to the hotel. Majesta was jealous of Courtney. *Just knowing that Nelson and my sister had intercourse and conceived a child really bothers me. But I'm trying to get past those feelings even though my family isn't making it easy for me.*

Things weren't exactly working out with Nelson either. He acted like he couldn't stand to touch Majesta since she'd become pregnant. She knew he was messing around.

Majesta would love it so much if he felt the love for her that she felt for him. The baby only made things worse for them. He wasn't happy when she told him of her pregnancy. In fact, he'd said, "You need to consider getting an abortion." But Majesta wasn't trying to hear that.

She thought about how lucky Courtney was to have a gorgeous guy like Steven. He seemed to genuinely care for her. She remembered how he was rubbing Courtney's flat stomach and holding her hand in the restaurant. Now Courtney had a degree and a much wanted baby.

Majesta and Nelson entered their hotel room and for what seemed like the one hundredth time, he would not have sex with her. She tried to place a kiss on his lips but Nelson turned his head. "What's wrong?" Majesta asked.

"Nothing," he replied, facing her again.

Holding his hand, Majesta pulled him close to her. She was hungry for his love. Kissing him, she reached down, and grabbed his manhood. Nelson didn't respond, he only kissed her on the cheek and stepped away.

Standing there looking at him with sadness on her face, Majesta blinked in disbelief. He didn't love her, and she didn't know if she could handle the rejection. Majesta climbed into the bed and cried herself to sleep. Nelson waited for her to start snoring, then he left the room and went to a local sport's bar.

Kim saw Nelson leaving the hotel as they arrived. Carlton noticed him before Kim did, but he didn't say a word. Nelson glanced at them as he drove by. They both wondered where he was going without Majesta.

Kim just shook her head. The twins had fallen asleep so she started waking them up. "Come on, you guys need to get up. We're back at the hotel."

Jeremy sat in the car seat eating a cookie while Carlton, Jr., was playing with his pocket game. They'd dropped off Kim's parents at Courtney's place.

Immediately, Kim went to see about her baby sister. She turned the doorknob and stepped into the room. *That dummy Nelson didn't even bother to close the door all the way. Anybody could have just walked in on my sister.* Kim saw that her sister was tired so she didn't try waking her up.

Kim's sister had infuriated her that morning. But she felt sorry for Majesta now as she watched her sleeping. Kim hated that they would be separated again. Majesta would go back to Texas with that jerk. *I wish that Majesta and Courtney would make up and put this terrible thing behind them.* Being the oldest, Kim felt that she should be the one to get them back on speaking terms.

Checking the door, Kim made sure that it was locked as she exited the room. For now, she would leave things alone.

Courtney enjoyed having her family in town. Jessica and the girls stayed a week. Courtney spent as much time as she could with them. Steven came over every evening for dinner. Jessica loved to cook so she made dinner for them nightly.

Courtney learned so much about babies that week. Mariah loved to talk so Courtney lent her an ear. She and Steven took Mariah to the mall and the movies twice. Jasmine was hard to get close to. She only let Courtney hold her once for about a minute. She was indeed a mama's baby.

When it was time for Jessie and the girls to return to Miami, Steven and Courtney drove them to the airport. They used Steven's Monte Carlo because Courtney's Chevette was too small.

This was a sad moment for Courtney and Jessica because they had really enjoyed each other's company. They hugged each other good-bye and shared parting words before Jessica boarded the plan with her children.

"I'm looking forward to you visiting me in Houston, sis."

"Yeah, it's going to be a lot of fun. You know, I enjoyed the talks we had every night after Steven left and the girls were asleep."

"I did, too. It was great having our sister dialogue until the early morning hour."

Once upon a time, all four sisters could talk like that. Majesta talked too much to outsiders. She had been telling Nelson all the sisters' secrets. Courtney hoped that her move to Texas would bring her and Majesta close again. She and Jessica often talked about that.

On the way back from the airport, Steven told Courtney, "I'm not sure if I can handle you moving to Texas." She was scheduled to leave in two weeks.

Courtney tried to speak, but tears flooded her eyes as the words got caught in her throat. She really didn't want to leave either.

Finally, she managed to say, "I don't know what to do. I've thought about putting law school on hold until the baby is born."

Steven replied, "I wouldn't dream of letting you do that. It's your dream, and you don't have a reason to put it on hold. Before you know it, the baby will be born, and I'll be with you once I get a transfer."

"Steven, don't transfer. I know that you want to graduate from Fayetteville State University. You only have one year left. We'll work this out with God's help."

He dropped Courtney off at her place because he had several errands to run. Courtney went straight to bed. She was tired; it seemed like the whole week of staying up late with her sister had caught up with her. She was asleep in no time flat.

A couple of weeks later, Courtney moved to Houston, Texas, to start classes at Thurgood Marshall's School of Law. Majesta helped her like she'd promised, and they started trying to communicate with each other again in a civilized manner.

While unpacking the dishes in the kitchen, Majesta spoke to her sister, "Courtney, I really wish you would try to understand why I stayed with Nelson."

"I don't think I'll ever be able to understand that."

"Well, I wish you'd at least try."

"Look, thanks for helping me out today, but let's not discuss him. You'll always be my sister. And that's all that matters to me."

Majesta replied, "Thanks, sis. I hope we can start rebuilding our relationship."

"Me, too."

Chapter eight

Courtney was almost six months pregnant in the fall and not really showing. Steven came to visit her regularly like he'd promised. He really liked Houston and was looking forward to moving there himself. They made such good love the times that he visited her. Lying in each other's arms, they would often talk about the baby.

Steven even gave Courtney an engagement ring on his last visit. She didn't think twice about marrying him. He was down on both knees when he proposed to her. Courtney said yes as fast as she could.

Like all the other visits, this one ended in tears. Since her pregnancy, Courtney cried about everything. She also asked Steven, "Could you please stop wearing that cologne. I used to be crazy about it but now I don't like it anymore."

"That's not a problem. I never really liked it anyway. I just wore it for you. I'll change anything that you want me to."

She also didn't like the smell of certain foods. But the two foods that Courtney really couldn't stand were onions and garlic. Just the thought of them would make her ill.

Smiling down at the beautiful ring on her finger, Courtney thought about her fiancé and wished that he was with her. She felt like a complete woman when Steven was around. This was her first time in a long distance relationship, and it was taking its toll on her.

It was good that she and Majesta were talking more and attending church together now. Courtney met a lot of interesting people there, including a very handsome guy. One Sunday, he had been smiling at her throughout the service. After church, he came over to her and introduced himself. "Hi, my name is Roger. I'm sorry for staring at you, but I'm delighted to meet you," he said, extending his right hand to her.

"Hello, I'm Courtney. The pleasure is all mine," she replied, shaking his hand. She noticed that he had a nice firm handshake. They shared a friendly conversation for several minutes and Courtney found out that he was also attending law school. She felt an attraction to him creeping through her bones when Roger asked, "Since you're new in town, I'd really like to show you a few places."

"I'll think about it."

"Well, here's my telephone number in case you decide to take me up on my offer," he replied, writing it down on her program booklet.

Courtney folded the paper and placed it in her purse. Nobody knew that she was pregnant except Majesta. It would be another month before she started to really show.

"He's a great guy," Majesta told Courtney as they exited the sanctuary. "He comes from a good family. Most of them belong to this congregation." But what she didn't say was that she was attracted to Roger, too.

Mrs. Williams, Roger's mother, invited them over for dinner. Roger had other plans, but when he found out that Courtney was going to be there, he cancelled them.

On the way over there, Courtney told Majesta, "Don't tell anyone about my pregnancy." She was worried about what Roger would think if he found out about her condition. Since she enjoyed his attention, Courtney didn't want to jeopardize this newfound friendship.

"Well, if that's what you want. My lips are sealed."

Courtney and Roger talked a lot after dinner that day. "So how are you enjoying your stay in Houston?"

"Things are moving along smoothly. I'm looking forward to school starting next month." She enjoyed the remainder of their conversation as they talked about everything from school to family.

By the end of the meal, Courtney and Roger felt like old friends. They were looking forward to meeting and talking again.

Courtney sat in bed eating Frosted Flakes cereal, a snack that she had every night before she went to sleep. At six months pregnant, she still wasn't fat. She had been walking around the Astrodome almost every day since arriving in Houston. Sometimes Roger would join her. He still liked her even though she'd told him about Steven and the baby.

"I should have known; all of the good women are taken," he said with a smile.

"I hope that we can still be friends."

Against his better judgment, he replied, "Of course we can. I could never have too many of those. Any time that you need to study, just give me a call."

Taking him up on his offer, Courtney called him and they got together almost every week. *I can't believe that I have two great guys in my life, one for a lover and one for a friend.* Roger was so good to her. One day, he asked, "Can I touch your stomach?"

"Sure," she replied, placing his palm over her belly button. After that, he would touch her stomach and talk to the baby whenever they met.

His mother loved to cook and bake goodies so Roger made sure that he brought Courtney treats almost every week. Courtney became very close to his family over these few months. They were good God-fearing people. Courtney was blessed that she'd met them through Majesta.

At bedtime, Courtney said her prayers and closed with, "Thank you, Father, for surrounding me with such wonderful people in a strange land." Then she drifted off to sleep thinking about Roger's family.

Early the next morning, the telephone rang. Courtney wiped her eyes and stared at the clock displaying six fifteen. Wondering who could be calling her this early she answered in a questioning tone, "Hello?"

"Courtney, it's Dr. Palmer."

With a strange feeling floating through her body, Courtney sat up in bed, leaning over on her side. It had always bothered her to get calls early in the morning while she was still sleepy. *Why is Steven's father calling me anyway?*

"How are you doing, Dr. Palmer? I miss you and Steven so much." Silence came over the telephone.

"Are you still there? Dr. Palmer, what's wrong? Is Steven all right?"

"Courtney, I have some very bad news and this is hard for me to tell you especially with you being pregnant. It only makes matters worse. Are you still in bed?"

"Please, Dr. Palmer, tell me what's wrong. Is Steven all right?" she asked again.

"No, Courtney. I'm sorry to tell you this, but Steven is dead."

Feeling her eyes become watery, Courtney couldn't stop the flow of tears overwhelming her. She leaned her body to the side and regurgitated in the middle of the bed. Dr. Palmer heard her sickness, and then he heard a loud moan escape her lips. He also heard the pain in her cry. The telephone hit the floor with a thud. Dr. Palmer was calling her name. "Courtney, answer me. Say something, Courtney."

She sat there in shock. Words ran through her mind, but they didn't cross her lips. *How can the father of my child be dead? What happened to Steven? Oh, God, what I am I going to do?*

Dr. Palmer hung the telephone up. He decided that it would be best to call her back later. It was really hard calling Courtney like that, but she needed to know. He had funeral arrangements to make and other family and friends to notify. *I wish that I could go to Courtney, but I can't leave the state right now.*

Steven had died instantly from massive head injuries sustained in an automobile accident. He lost control of the vehicle on a wet road and ran into a light pole. His dad decided that he would have a closed casket funeral.

Courtney hung up the telephone when she heard the dial tone. Sitting up in bed, she could no longer stand the smell of her vomit. She prayed that it was just a bad dream.

Pulling her sheets off the bed, she went to put them in the bathroom. Courtney took small steps toward the clothes hamper, praying for this nightmare to end.

Fumbling to the living room, she dialed Steven's number. The telephone rang four times, then Steven's voice machine came on. At first Courtney got excited because the message began with a hello. But when she realized it was a machine she choked up. She left a message saying, "Steven, it's Courtney. I love you." That was all she managed to get out as she gripped her stomach, fighting the tears streaming down her face.

At seven o'clock, Courtney received another telephone call from Dr. Palmer. They talked and cried for almost an hour. It was such a great lost for both of them.

"Listen, Courtney, I'll make the arrangements for you to fly up here. You can stay with me. And promise me that you'll bring the baby to see me when it's born."

"Yes, I promise to bring your grandson, to see you," she said, swallowing her tears. It was becoming too painful for her to talk. "I'm going to call you back later. I have to go now."

"I understand. I'm looking forward to seeing you soon. Go get you some rest for now."

Attending Steven's funeral was the hardest thing that Courtney had ever done. She sat next to his father as if she was his widow. There were many students from the university and Steven had such a large family in attendance.

Dr. Palmer was the fourth born of seven children. They all made it to the funeral except for his brother, Stanley, who was out of the country on business. Stanley traveled extensively; it was hard to keep up with where he was or who he was with for that matter.

On the second Saturday in November, The New Grove Baptist Church was full of flowers and plant arrangements. The program was a light blue with black print. Inside the front cover was a handsome picture of Steven.

On the program, Courtney's name was listed as being the fiancé with child along with a host of family and friends. Courtney felt shaken. The tears ran down her face like a never-ending waterfall.

Dr. Palmer held Courtney's hand throughout the short service. At the end of the ceremony, six of Steven's closest friends carried him out of the church while the choir sang, "I'll Fly Away."

Courtney came close to fainting, but she fought it with all her might. It didn't help that three other women did pass out during the service. Her throat was sore, her stomach hurt, and she felt nauseous. She was trying to control herself, but Courtney felt like running straight out of the church, screaming all the way to the cemetery.

Steven was laid to rest next to his mother in a well kept cemetery not very far from the church. Riding in the back of the limousine with Dr. Palmer, Courtney wept the entire way. With his arms around her shoulders, Dr. Palmer comforted her the best that he could.

Once they were home, Courtney decided to retire to her designated room. She couldn't deal with being around a lot of folks that she didn't know right now. Most of the attendees had followed them back to Dr. Palmer's house where they planned to serve dinner.

Two days later, Courtney left North Carolina and headed back to Houston. Before leaving, she promised Dr. Palmer, "I'll be back to see you when the baby's old enough to travel."

"I'd love that. I'm counting on you to keep your word. I can't wait to see my grandson."

"I want my son to know his wonderful grandfather."

"Well, the two of you are all I've got so please keep in touch."

Stepping off the airplane, Courtney was surprised to see her three sisters all waiting with open arms to greet her. Majesta had told Jessica and Kim about Steven's death. Jessica had planned to spend some time in Houston with her sister anyway. She just decided to do it sooner. Kim left her boys with Carlton.

Jessica was holding Jasmine while Kim held on to Mariah's hand. Crying as she walked towards her family, Courtney thought her heart would burst. The sisters circled Courtney, giving her a group hug, telling her how sorry they were.

Majesta said, "I know you're hurting, but Mrs. Williams said that she wanted to see you when you arrived back in town. Would you like to go by her house for awhile?"

Courtney really liked the outgoing fifty-five-year-old woman who acted a lot younger. So although she didn't feel like doing anything except going home to sleep, she replied, "Yes, that'll be fine." The only time that she had true peace was in her sleep. She found it hard to get up in the morning facing another day knowing that the love of her life was gone.

When Mrs. Williams heard the car pull into the driveway, she stood to see who it was. "Oh, it's Courtney and her sisters."

Majesta had brought them over the day before and introduced them to Mrs. Williams. They all adored the older lady. She gladly welcomed them into her home again.

Roger had his own place but often spent time at his mom's house, especially in her kitchen. He was sleeping on the sofa in the family room. "Roger get up, son. They're here."

Getting up, Roger went to the bathroom and quickly washed his face. He had missed Courtney. Now he realized how much he cared for her. He felt guilty for wanting Courtney, but he was planning to win her heart by taking the slow and steady route.

Majesta was very beautiful to Roger. He'd even noticed the seductive looks that she'd given him but figured that it was just a physical attraction with her. She had offered herself with her eyes so many times that he'd lost count. *The last thing I need to do is come between two sisters. I'm glad that I never went after Majesta even though I met her a year before Courtney.*

As Roger entered the living room, Courtney and her sisters were sitting on the couch. Majesta stood, introduced Kim and Jessica to Roger. Courtney spoke to him, and then turned to look out the window.

Reaching out to Courtney, Roger gently wrapped his arms around her in a warm embrace. "Hi, Courtney, it's good to see you."

Mrs. Williams knelt down next to Courtney, held her hand, and said a soft prayer. She shared with them how she'd lost her husband when her kids were young. "Baby, just take one day at a time and remember that we have a God that can fix anything, even a broken heart. You are surrounded by so many people who love you. It's so sweet of your sisters to come and be with you at a time like this. I wish my kids could be like that. They live in the same state and they see each other every blue moon. Anytime you want to talk to someone, call me, okay?"

Majesta went into Mrs. Williams' bedroom to check on Ah'Shiyah, her beautiful baby girl, who was still asleep. If it wasn't for Courtney and Mrs. Williams, she didn't know what she would have done, especially since Nelson had stopped coming by to see her. He even claimed that he didn't believe that the baby was his. Majesta let him go because she was finally sick of his trifling ways. Yet, it was hard to admit that she'd made a mistake.

Majesta was really thinking about transferring to another college. University of Miami was all right. She knew a lot of people who went to school there. And sometimes she wished that she was around her parents.

As she watched Ah'Shiyah sleeping peacefully on her stomach, Majesta wondered how she would grow up. Ah'Shiyah wasn't quite two month olds, but she was already plump with dark skin like Majesta and curly coal black hair.

She was so proud of her baby girl. When Nelson left her during the middle of her pregnancy, Majesta wished for the baby to be a girl. *It would be nice for her to have a father that loves her. I see how Roger looks at Courtney. Even though she's pregnant with another man's child, he has feelings for her. I've been trying to get close to him, but he's just not interested in me. He's such a sweet guy. I know he'd make a great husband and father.*

Majesta even tried using the baby to get closer to Roger. Once she asked him to watch Ah'Shiyah just to see if he would. The baby was just two weeks old. She asked him to come to her apartment so that she could run to the store for a minute. Roger admitted that he was a little nervous about keeping a newborn, but he agreed to come over.

"Hi, Roger, come on in. The baby's sleeping."

He stepped into the living room wearing a strange look on his face. "Hello, Majesta."

"Thanks for coming over," she replied, meeting him at the door in her purple nightie.

Looking her up and down, he asked, "What's going on, Majesta? Why aren't you dressed yet?"

"Because I was waiting on you to get here. Why? Don't you like what I have on?"

"It's…" He couldn't get the words out. Majesta had pressed her chest against his and covered his mouth with hers.

Pulling away, Roger asked, "What are you doing? Never mind. I'm out of here." He walked out of the apartment just as fast as he walked in.

"Damn," Majesta sighed, slamming the door behind him. She was frustrated with the fact that her seduction plan had failed.

Majesta knew that Courtney was still in love with Steven. He was all that she ever talked about. Majesta had asked Courtney to live with her when she first moved to Houston, but her sister had gotten used to living alone and turned her down. She laughed saying, "Steven is the only person that I want to live with." It was hard to believe that he was dead.

When Nelson walked out on Majesta, she felt sorry for herself. Now she was hoping that one day he would return. *There's still hope. My daughter needs her daddy.*

Kissing her baby, Majesta patted her on the back, and returned to the living room with the others. Jessica was in the kitchen with Mrs. Williams who had Mariah on her lap. Jasmine was on the couch asleep. Kim was in the living room next to Jasmine talking to Roger. "Where is Courtney?" she asked Kim.

"She's in the bathroom."

"So, Roger, what you been up to?" Majesta asked, turning to face him.

"Oh, I've been studying a lot. I'm worried about Courtney."

"Do you think she can continue law school in her state of mind?"

"I told her that I would help in anyway. I was just telling Kim how much I care for Courtney. I told Courtney that I would always be there for her."

They stopped speaking when Courtney entered the room. She sat on the couch looking bored. Roger stood up and said, "It was great seeing you all, but I have to go now."

He walked over to Courtney, taking her by the hand. "Give me a call if you want to talk later. I'm just a telephone call away. Once again, I'm sorry about your loss."

"Thank you, Roger."

Bending down, Roger hugged Courtney around the neck. Then he went to the kitchen and kissed his mother good-bye.

Majesta noticed how Roger looked at Courtney with pity in his eyes. She knew then and there that he wanted her sister. It seemed like Courtney was finally getting some decent guys. She'd started out with some thoughtless low-down men. Alex really broke her heart. The family thought that she was going to die without him. And then what she went through with Nelson was horrible.

Jessica entered the living room, looked at Courtney, and she knew that her sister was ready to go, too. She turned around when Mrs. Williams asked, "Would you all like to stay for dinner?"

They answered, "No, thank you." However, they did decide to take plates of fried catfish, potato salad, string beans, homemade butter milk biscuits, and homemade tartar sauce with them. For dessert, she made a five flavor pound cake and a key lime pie. Mrs. Williams fixed a hefty plate for Courtney and said, "I want you to eat every bite."

Courtney simply nodded her head as Mrs. Williams continued, "Feed that baby, Courtney, and if you want to eat anything else just call me, and I'll fix it for you and have Roger bring it over."

Taking the plate, Courtney gave Mrs. Williams a kiss on the cheek and said, "Thank you so much."

Everyone camped out at Courtney's apartment. When they got there, Courtney went to bed. Kim, Jessica, and Majesta sat up all night eating and talking about old times. "I wish this hadn't happened to Courtney, she is a mess. I don't think she had anything to eat today."

"I know, Kim, she usually eats really well. When I was pregnant with Ah'Shiyah, we were always eating. Mrs. Williams was always cooking and sending food over here by Roger."

Jessie said, "Majesta, when I was in the kitchen with Mrs. Williams, Roger told me that he liked Courtney. Does he have a girlfriend?"

"No, but I've been trying to be his girlfriend since I met him in church. I was pregnant and Nelson was acting mean to me. I was really lonely. When Roger smiled at me and asked when I was due, I just melted. He's smooth, my sisters, real smooth. And he got looks and has brains to match."

Kim interjected, "I noticed how he only looked at Courtney with those brown eyes of his."

"Yeah, I know he wants her. I just have to live with that," Majesta said, knowing that she didn't stand a chance at gaining Roger's attention.

Roger had two brothers and two sisters. His sister, Samantha, told Majesta, "My brother's single. If you're attracted to him, then let him know. It doesn't matter that you're pregnant."

But apparently, Majesta wasn't the pregnant sister that he wanted. And he'd made that clear to each of them.

When Courtney woke up, she smelled bacon cooking. Jessica had gotten up earlier and made a big breakfast including pancakes, turkey bacon, eggs, grits, and biscuits.

Courtney promised herself that she would never have a serious relationship again. She would only have time for the child that was growing inside her.

Kim knocked on the bedroom door, stuck her head in, and asked, "Courtney, are you awake? Come eat some breakfast. Jessica made you some grits and eggs. Majesta told her that you like that."

"I'm not hungry. I feel sick to my stomach."

Kim walked on into the room, sat on the bed, and looked at her sister. Courtney's eyes were puffy. She looked weak and pale. "I'm really worried about you. The reason you're sick is because you haven't been eating, sweetheart. You need to eat something for the baby."

Kim helped Courtney to the bathroom, and then she made up the bed for her. She and Courtney walked to the kitchen where everyone else was eating. Majesta and Ah'Shiyah had slept in the guest room. Jessica, her girls, and Kim slept in the living room on the carpeted floor. Jessica had a warm plate of grits and eggs waiting for her sister. She asked Courtney, "What type of juice would you like?"

Courtney didn't reply; she just stared at the plate. Kim looked at Jessica, shaking her head. Their sister was a basket case this morning. Jessica said, "Eat your food, Courtney, before it gets cold. Feed your baby. It only eats when you do."

Kim sat in the chair in front of Courtney and picked up the fork. She mixed the eggs and grits together then offered to feed her sister. Courtney slowly opened her mouth with tears flowing down her face. She was feeling real bad. There wasn't a happy bone in her body. Kim and Jessica knew this was going to be hard, but Courtney was in God's hands now.

After Kim got Courtney to eat a little, Courtney went to take a warm bath. Kim and Jessica talked about Courtney's state of mind while they cleaned the kitchen. Majesta walked in the kitchen with Ah'Shiyah in her arms and asked, "Where's Courtney?"

Kim said, "She's taking a bath. While you and Jessica were asleep last night, mama and daddy called and talked to Courtney. She cried the whole time she was on the telephone with them."

Soaking in the tub, Courtney could feel her baby moving. She thought about how pleasant Roger had been to her. *I know he likes me. There's no way that I could ever feel the same about him. I just want Steven back.*

She smiled as she felt the baby moving again. *At least I have a part of Steven inside of me.*

Courtney finished her bath, got dressed, and went to the kitchen to join her sisters. They were sitting at the table carrying on a conversation.

"Hi, baby, what do you want to do today?"

"Nothing, Kim, I'm not in the mood."

"Let's go to the mall. Majesta and Jessie want to have some pictures taken of the girls. Come on, it'll be fun to hang out," Kim said, touching her sister's arm.

"Okay, I'll go, but I'm really not in the mood to do anything."

"Roger called to see how you're doing. He also said that Mrs. Williams made a banana pudding for you."

"I don't want anything to eat. She's always cooking something."

"She's a sweet woman, Courtney."

"I know, Kim, but the last thing I want is something to eat."

"All right, then. Let's finish getting dressed and head to the mall," Kim replied, standing up.

While shopping, Kim bought Courtney some pretty leather sandals. Jessica bought her two maternity outfits. Courtney really didn't need anymore maternity clothes because Majesta had given her most of hers after Ah'Shiyah was born.

Jessica and Majesta went to the Children's Shop to find the girls something to wear for their pictures. Jessica found the same outfit for all three children. After being at the mall for two hours, they took the girls for pictures, and then left.

Kim suggested, "Let's go by Mrs. Williams house and pick up the banana pudding she made for Courtney."

Majesta replied, "That sounds good. I love her desserts."

They stayed at Mrs. Williams place for about an hour. Then they headed back to Courtney's apartment. Jessica couldn't wait to stick a spoon in the banana pudding.

"Courtney would you like to taste some? I mean, she did make it for you."

"No, maybe later."

Trying to cheer up her sister, Kim asked, "Where is your picture collection?"

"In some boxes in the closet of my bedroom. I really don't feel like setting them up."

"Well, maybe I can help you look through some of the pictures later if you don't mind."

"Maybe, sis. I just need to rest for now," Courtney replied, taking a seat on the sofa.

Jessica started dinner as soon as they returned. She fried some chicken, and made string beans with macaroni and cheese. Courtney finally tried a little banana pudding, but she didn't eat anything else.

Majesta pulled a movie out of Courtney's collection. She picked out one of her favorite movies, "Imitation of Life," that Kim hadn't seen before.

At the end of the movie, all four sisters had red eyes from weeping. "That's one of the best movies that I've ever seen," Kim said, reaching for a Kleenex tissue. She blew her nose as the other sisters nodded their heads in agreement.

Courtney said, "That movie always make me cry. I like this version better than the original version, but they're both good."

"I'm going to buy me a copy when I get back home. That's a classic," Jessica added.

Kim noticed that Courtney wasn't taking care of her hair. "Why don't you let me put some braids in your hair, sis?"

"Could you wash it, condition it, and put a French braid in it?"

"Ok, sis, that shouldn't take too long. You want me to do it now?"

"Yes, if you feel like it."

Kim washed, conditioned, and braided Courtney's natural hair like she said she would. It looked attractive on her.

Jessica was in the kitchen putting away the dishes while Kim put the finishing touches on Courtney's hairstyle. Majesta was in the living room with the girls watching a children's show. She sat with Ah'Shiyah in her lap. Ah'Shiyah even seemed to enjoy the show as well as her cousins.

Once the program was over, Jessica put Mariah and Jasmine in the bathtub. "I want to call my daddy," Mariah said.

The last thing Jessica wanted to do was call William. He had been so distant. The only reason he stayed with her was the girls. In fact, he'd only called them once since they'd left. Her parents had found her a lawyer. She planned to grant his divorce wish.

Jessica thought about Paul Taylor, the guy from high school that she'd run into before leaving town. He had given her his telephone number and asked her to keep in touch. Jessica called him and they met for lunch. Paul was handsome with thick eyebrows over sexy eyes. It really surprised Jessie that he was interested in her. He kept himself in shape. And after listening to her make several comments about her weight, Paul talked her into visiting the spa that he attended.

At the restaurant, Paul said, "You can visit as my guest to see if you like it."

Before Jessica responded with a yes, she made sure that it wasn't the gym that William attended. Luckily, it wasn't so they made plans to meet there. *This is great. Maybe I'll be able to lose some weight. Paul seems like a patient guy.*

"Jessie, I noticed that you've barely eaten anything. Are you dieting?"

"Ah, yes, I am. I need to lose a few pounds. I gained so much weight in the last year."

"Well, I think it looks appealing on you. Besides, dieting is not a good idea. It's best to take it off with exercise."

"I know."

"Diets are temporary. Just cut out fatty foods and try to prepare you own meals instead of eating out. Drink lots of water when you eat and exercise more. You can start off with power walking at the spa."

"Thanks for the information. I'll give it a try."

"I have another tip for you. Stop eating after seven o'clock in the evening. If you get hungry before you go to bed, just eat some fruit or bran cereal with skim milk."

Taking his advice, Jessica was already starting to lose weight at a surprising rate. She was drinking more water and doing floor exercise nightly before going to bed. Things were looking optimistic for her, and she planned to keep it up.

When she finished bathing the girls, Jessica let them call their daddy. She was shocked to find him home. "Hello."

"Hi, William, the girls wanted to talk to you before they went to bed. Hold on."

Jessica put Jasmine on the telephone. "Hi, daddy loves you Jazzie Poo," William cooed to his baby girl.

Mariah had lots to talk about. "Daddy, we went to the mall today. This lady, Mrs. Williams made a banana pudding. Daddy, it tastes so good. I'm going to bring you some, okay?"

She went on and on. Mariah even told her daddy about how Aunt Courtney cried too much and how she looked sad all the time. "Okay, baby, that's enough," Jessie said, taking the telephone from Mariah.

After putting the girls to bed, Jessica thought about that banana pudding that Mrs. Williams made. It was delicious. She'd had some earlier but wanted more now. Majesta was already in the kitchen devouring it. Jessie got a small bowl and joined her sister.

"Girl, this is some good banana pudding. We got to ask her for the recipe."

"Girl, are you crazy? I'm not going to take any back with me or the recipe. I'm trying to watch my weight. But this is too good to resist while I'm here."

"Sho' you right."

Courtney walked into the kitchen and joined her sisters. They sat at the table talking for hours about their lives and dreams.

Courtney didn't eat, but she finally called it a day around midnight and went to bed. Majesta and Ah'Shiyah also retired for the evening. Kim wasn't sleepy so she looked into Courtney's video collection for a tape to watch. She found the best of the "I Love Lucy" series.

They used to love watching the zany Lucy as kids. Kim sat up watching different episodes, trying not to laugh out loud and disturb her sister and nieces. Jessica didn't feel like pulling out the sofa bed so she and the girls crashed on the floor in the corner away from the TV set.

Courtney tossed and turned in her sleep. She was having a bad dream about the baby. She could see the child being born. The doctor and nurses surrounded her hospital bed with solemn looks on their faces. The room was deathly quiet. "What's wrong with my baby? Why isn't he crying? Why isn't he moving?"

She woke up sweating, crying, and grabbing her belly to feel the baby kicking. It was two o'clock in the morning. Courtney went to the bathroom, brushed her teeth, and washed her face. Then she went to the refrigerator for some more banana pudding knowing that she would pay for it later. Tomorrow she would have to call Mrs. Williams to thank her for her generosity.

Sitting at the table, Courtney thought about her dreams. *Oh, how I miss Steven. He was the only man who made me forget about Alex. I wonder what Alex is doing these days. But at least Steven left me something behind to cherish forever more.* Courtney rubbed her hands across her belly as she thought of Steven.

Kim saw the kitchen light on so she went to see who was in there. She was happy to find Courtney sitting at the table eating.

"Hi, sis, are you okay?"

"I'm all right. I just had a bad dream and had to get up. Thanks for asking."

"No, problem. What are sisters for?" Kim asked, thinking, *Maybe she'll be all right with time. I'll be sure to keep in touch with her when I return to Miami. Courtney needs her sisters more than ever now. Even Majesta seems to be closer to her now that Nelson is out of the picture. I'm sure that he'll be back as soon as she finds someone else. But I hope she never takes that rapist jerk back. God, please bless my sisters*, she prayed silently.

Chapter nine

Being in labor for several hours left Courtney exhausted. She was determined to have her baby naturally, but it was getting hard to tolerate the pain.

She called Roger before leaving home in a taxi and Roger had called Majesta, but she wasn't home. He rushed to the hospital to be by her side. Right now, Roger was holding Courtney's hand, feeling each contraction as it occurred.

"Roger, I feel another one. It hurts. Ah! Ah! Ah!"

"Breathe, Courtney, don't tense up, breathe!"

Seven hours later, she had dilated eight centimeters. Roger said, "It won't be long now." He was already acting like a daddy.

"Today's my birthday," Dr. Grace Perkins, a middle aged African American woman wearing a short jerri-curl said. "It looks like it's going to be your baby's birthday, too."

Responding with another loud scream, Courtney squeezed Roger's hand as hard as she could. She was ready for this baby to be born.

"Come on, Courtney, it's time to push. This baby will be born on my fifty-seventh birthday." Giving her a tired smile, Courtney sat up into a pushing position.

"Push, Courtney!" Roger and Dr. Perkins both screamed. Roger held Courtncy's shaking hands as she pushed harder. Courtney could feel the pain with each strong contraction. It felt like she was pushing something out that should be cut out of her stomach.

On February 1, 1992, the baby tore Courtney's vagina as he entered the world, requiring her to have an episiotomy, weighing nine pounds and thirteen ounces. Courtney was seeing stars as she laid her head on the sweat soaked pillow. Roger kissed her on the cheek. "I love you," he whispered into her ear.

Courtney mouthed, "I love you, Roger."

They had become close during the months preceding the birth. Spending lots of time together studying at his place, she'd come to love Roger, too.

On one occasion, Courtney had been sitting on the floor rubbing her stomach. Roger knelt down next to her and placed his hands on her stomach, too. Courtney felt a chill run through her body just from his touch. She could see the longing in his eyes as he held her hand. It had been months since she'd had sex.

Roger kissed her lips, rubbing her tender breasts. Courtney felt warmth all over. She slowly removed her shirt, then her bra revealing her pregnancy in all its beauty. Roger looked into Courtney's face which was still just as pretty as it was when they'd first met. Her breasts were large as balloons. She looked like she could deliver any day.

Lying her down ever so gently on a pillow, Roger removed his shirt and was thinking, *I'm not sure that this is a good idea, but it feels right. I just have to be gentle with her.*

Courtney wanted him just as much. She helped him remove the rest of his clothing as he lay down close to her. With her back to him, Courtney felt safe.

Holding her with his hands on her large belly, she felt his manhood against her backside. "It'll be better to make love in this position. My stomach is too big to do it any other way."

"Are you sure, Courtney? I can wait until after the baby is born."

"Roger, make love to me. I need your love. I need for us to connect."

He responded by kissing the back of her neck. Then he was as gentle with her as he could be. When they were finished, they lay on the floor and slept the remainder of the day. That was the only time they'd physically connected.

Reminding Courtney of where she was, Nurse Benson asked, "Are you planning to breast feed?"

"Yes. Can I hold him?"

The nurse handed Steven Roger to his mother. "You can nurse him now if you like."

Courtney looked at the baby. He was so big, sucking on his fist. He looked just like Steven even though he was light skinned now; his ears were dark and he had a head full of curly hair. He would probably be dark like his father.

As Courtney looked at Roger, she realized that the baby could easily pass for his son. He helped Courtney untie her gown so that she could nurse the baby.

Feeling a little bit of pain as she nursed, Courtney's abdomen cramped, and she felt blood flowing heavily from her vaginal area. Her breasts were hurting bad; she wanted to remove one from the baby's mouth, but he had latched on well. She just kissed him on the head and looked up at Roger.

"Nurse, I'm really in pain here."

"All right, let me help you up. Do you need to use the bathroom?"

"Yes, ma'am, my bladder is full."

The nurse placed the baby in the crib and helped Courtney to the restroom. She was a bloody mess. Her gown was soaked through.

Roger felt sorry for her as she walked ever so slowly to the bathroom. The nurse helped her to the toilet and handed Courtney a sanitary napkin with netted underwear.

While she was urinating, she felt some relief. Nurse Benson changed Courtney's sheets and changed the birthing bed into a hospital bed.

When Courtney returned to the bed, Roger stood by her side and said, "I'm tired. I think I'll leave and come back in the morning."

"Don't leave, Roger. You can spend the night. It's all right."

"Okay, sweetheart, anything for you."

"Would you like to hold your son?"

"Courtney, what do you mean my son?"

"Roger, will you marry me? I love you, and I want you to help me raise Steven Roger."

"I love you, too, Courtney. You know, I asked you to marry me months ago, but you never gave me an answer."

"Yes, I know. I just needed time to think about it. Here, hold your son. I want to call him Lil' Roger. What do you think about that?"

Roger couldn't hide the smile that crossed his face. "Sure, I like the way it sounds."

Courtney handed him the baby. Roger rocked his son to sleep. Then Nurse Benson took the baby and placed him back in the crib.

As soon as the nurse left the room, someone came in from the cafeteria. Courtney and Roger were both hungry. It really didn't matter what was on the menu as long as it was edible.

After lunch, they both fell asleep. At 4:00 p.m., they were both awakened by Lil' Roger. Courtney got up, realizing that she was a bloody mess again. She changed herself, washed her hands and nipples, then got the baby and nursed him.

"Roger, could you hand me a Pamper, wipes, and an alcohol pad?"

"Okay."

She changed the baby, and patted his cord with the alcohol pad to dry it up. Touching his cord made her nervous. She had heard stories about a baby's cord and how delicate it could be, and that if anyone pulled it off, the baby would bleed to death. Courtney didn't know how true that was, but she didn't want to take any chances.

"The cord will fall off in seven to eight days," the nurse said.

"I'm just concerned about my baby."

"And that's perfectly understandable. Don't worry," the nurse said with a knowing smile as she left the room, leaving Courtney and Roger alone with the child.

"Roger, I promised Dr. Palmer I would bring his grandson to see him. I know Lil' Roger is not old enough to travel right now but would you consider going with us when we're ready?"

"I don't think that's a good idea. I need to focus on law school for a while. And we've got to get you back on track. I'll be graduating soon, but you still have two years left."

Majesta finally came to the hospital around eleven o'clock that morning. She walked in to see Roger sitting by Courtney's side. "Hi, mama," she said to Courtney.

"Majesta, I'm glad you finally made it. Have you called everyone?"

"Not yet, I wanted to see you and the baby first, sis. You know, they're going to want to know all the details. How you look and how the baby looks. I'll call them when I get home."

"Excuse me," Roger interrupted and stood up. "I'm going to get a snack and let you ladies chat for a minute." He leaned over and planted a kiss on Courtney's forehead.

Courtney looked into his eyes and mouthed, "Thank you."

Roger nodded his head, walked to the door, and stopped. He glanced back at Courtney one time before walking out the door.

Majesta went over to see her nephew. "He's so cute. He looks like he could be Roger's son."

"Girl, you're crazy."

"No, I'm not. You always like dark skinned men. Alex was brown skinned but all the rest were dark." *Including Nelson.*

"Can I hold my nephew, please?" Majesta asked, eyeing her sister for a response.

"Wash your hands first."

"I know, Ms. Clean Thang."

Majesta smiled as she went to the sink and washed her hands. Then she walked over to the sleeping baby, carefully picking him up. She sat on the couch with the baby cradled in her arms.

"He's so cute. Look at his curly hair. I could hold him for hours."

Minutes passed before Courtney said, "Roger and I are planning to get married when Lil' Roger turns one. We don't want to rush into anything."

Just then, Roger returned and sat on the bed smiling at the two women. He was always in a good mood. Majesta thought, *I can't ever remember seeing him in a bad mood. I wonder if he's for real. There might be another side to Mr. Roger.*

"Congratulations to both of you." Majesta really didn't like the news, but she just played it off.

Placing Lil' Roger back in the bed, she said, "I may be moving back to Miami. You know, I have more friends there. I wish I could find a man to love me and my baby. Maybe my Mr. Right's in Miami."

"Maybe he is, sis. Maybe he is."

Courtney was happy to be discharged from the hospital. The nurse pushed her and Lil' Roger out of the room in a wheelchair. Roger pulled up in the car and helped them in. Lil' Roger lay in his car seat, sleeping the entire way home.

Feeling sick, Courtney asked, "Roger, can we please hurry home?"

"What's wrong, baby?"

"I'm just not feeling well."

"Would you like to go back to the hospital?"

"Oh, no, I'm too happy to be out of that place. I just need to get home and relax."

Roger made it to the apartment in fifteen minutes. Courtney was feeling bad. Her stitches from the episiotomy and her hard breasts were giving her the blues. She felt like crying. *I wish I had that wheelchair from the hospital. Now I feel a headache coming on. I need to feed the baby to relieve my throbbing breasts.*

"I'm not having anymore babies."

"We're going to have us a little girl. Wouldn't you like that?"

"We'll have to talk about that when Lil' Roger turns five years old, okay?"

Slowly, Courtney walked into her apartment while Roger got their son out of the car seat. Entering her clean apartment, she smiled to herself. Roger had everything just like she'd left it. He had finished the baby room that she'd started decorating.

Those last few days before delivery had been hard. She just couldn't get comfortable. Roger had done all he could to make her happy, but nothing seemed to work.

When she walked in the living room, Roger placed some pillows on the sofa so that she could sit on them. He laid Lil' Roger in the crib and went back to the car for her hospital things including the gifts that she'd received for the baby. Courtney smiled even though she was in pain.

"Roger, could you bring the baby to me, please?"

He nodded and did as she asked. As soon as the baby was in Courtney's arms, she unfastened her shirt and started nursing him. She didn't even bother to wipe off her nipples. Courtney needed relief that only Lil' Roger could provide.

Turning his head to her breast, the baby started sucking. He opened his eyes, looking at Courtney with his hands in fists. At first she felt pain, and then relief. She enjoyed the process more once the pain was gone. Courtney had always said that she would breast feed her children. She'd heard that it was good for the mom's figure, and she was ready to get in shape. She and Roger planned to start walking and then try jogging.

Roger sat on the couch watching Courtney painfully nurse the baby. He was proud of his sweetheart.

Rubbing the baby's curly hair, he noticed the resemblance to himself. He asked Courtney several questions about the baby's father, and she responded with tears. "He would be so proud. I really loved him, Roger. He was a good person."

"I love you, and I love our baby. We're going to be a family, that's if you still want me."

"Of course, I do. I love you, too. God is good, and I thank him for you."

Courtney finished nursing the baby, burped him, and handed him to Roger. Then she crept to the bathroom, turning on the warm water in the tub. She bled heavily every time she nursed her baby and couldn't wait to clean up herself.

Courtney took off her blood soaked underwear and washed them in the sink in cold water. Picking up a hand mirror, she looked at her vaginal stitches in the mirror. *It looks ugly down there. Roger probably wouldn't bother with me if he saw that.*

Once the tub was full, she eased in. Although painful at first, the warmth soon felt soothing. She just sat in the bathtub adding hot water as the water cooled.

Looking at her large breast drooping over her stomach, she thought, *Boy, my body looks a hot mess.*

After her bath, Courtney pulled on some clean underwear. Because she was bleeding so heavily, she felt like she needed to wear a Pamper just like her baby.

Entering the bedroom, she saw Roger lying in bed with Lil' Roger next to him. He was asleep with his hand touching the baby. *Oh, they're so cute together. He's going to be a great dad.*

Courtney found her camera, took a picture of them, and then she took a nap. At eight o'clock that night, Courtney's parents called with Jessica and Kim on the line. They did three-way calls all the time.

"Hello."

"Congratulations!" they sang in chorus.

"Hi, everybody. I'm tired. My whole body hurts."

Kim asked, "Where's Majesta? She's not there with you?"

"No, she came by the hospital, but I haven't seen her since I've been home. Roger is here with me though. He's been here the whole time."

"That's wonderful, sweetheart. Tell him that I said hi."

Since Courtney sounded really tired, they only talked for a few more minutes. She had to reassure them that all was well.

Moments later, Courtney was nursing her baby, again. Then she cleaned her stitches and changed her pad in the bathroom with the door opened. That's when she heard Roger talking to the baby. "Hi, man. Daddy loves that baby."

Roger was such a dear. All he did was lavish her with love and attention. *I believe that he might love me more than Steven did, but he doesn't know me like Steven knew me. I told Steven everything. One day, I'll tell Roger everything so that he can decide if he really wants to be with me.*

Carefully, Courtney returned to the bed. She wanted to make sure that she didn't tear her stitches. For some reason, she was thinking about Roger and his family a lot lately. She needed to know more about them.

"Roger, how did your father die?"

"Well, the man who raised me wasn't really my father."

Mrs. Williams had told Courtney that her husband was dead, and she thought he was Roger's daddy. Now she was learning the truth.

"My dad is still alive somewhere. My mother is from North Carolina. While she was a senior in high school, she got pregnant and dropped out. My dad denied getting her pregnant and went off to college somewhere."

"Do you know his name?"

"Nah, my mom wouldn't even tell me that. But I did hear her tell my Aunt Shirley one time that I looked like my daddy, Kool-Aid. So I guess that's his nickname or something."

"I want my baby to know about his daddy's family. I don't want any secrets. Secrets cause trouble in the long run. I had been living with a secret and it almost caused me to kill myself. I think your mother should tell you about your father, you're old enough now. When I take Lil' Roger to see his grandfather, you really should come with us."

"We'll see. I need to get back to my studies. I'll find my dad someday. I'm not worried about it."

This conversation prompted Courtney to doing some serious thinking. She was glad that she'd waited on marriage. She and Roger needed to get to know each other better. Maybe she could help him find his daddy. Maybe Dr. Palmer knew about Kool-Aid.

That night, Courtney called Dr. Palmer, telling him about his grandson. She said, "Lil' Roger weighed nine pounds and thirteen ounces at birth. He was definitely a big baby."

He told her, "Big babies run in our family."

"I'm bringing him out to see you as soon as we're well enough to travel."

"Good, you can stay here in Steven's old room. I'd like that."

"Okay, it would be good for the baby to be in a room filled with memories of his father."

"Yeah, we kept Steven's room exactly the way he left it. When he gets older, the baby will love my son's collection of miniature trucks, cars, and airplanes."

"Dr. Palmer, I really miss Steven. I really want to make an effort to keep in touch with you."

"I'm looking forward to it. I want to know my grandson. Are you coming alone?"

"Yes, sir, I am. I was planning to bring a friend, but that's okay." Courtney felt sad that Roger wasn't traveling with her since she decided to stay with Dr. Palmer, but she understood his position. *It definitely wouldn't be the ideal situation.*

Roger was beginning to wonder if Courtney was really over Steven and in love with him. *It's only been three months. How could she be over Steven?*

Then Roger thought about Majesta. *She keeps flirting with me. I don't understand what's wrong with her. Can't she see that I want Courtney?*

He knew Majesta was using Ah'Shiyah to hang around his family. His sister, Samantha, told him, "Majesta is talking about getting with you when Courtney is done."

"Yeah, well, she's crazy if you ask me."

"Majesta said that Courtney is the one with mental problems. She said Courtney has a minor case of OCD. And she told me that her boyfriend raped Courtney and got her pregnant."

"I know all of that, so what are you trying to say?"

"Roger, the girl's got secrets, and she's got problems. Have you seen her collages?"

"No, why?"

"Majesta said she does that when she's troubled. So watch out, brother. Get to know her before you marry her."

Courtney finally opened up to Roger and told him about her difficult past and how she loved creating collages. He'd never seen them, but Roger had seen eight boxes in the walk-in closet in the guest bedroom. Courtney told him, "One day, I'm going to redo my picture room."

He asked, "What's a picture collage?"

"You've never seen one?"

"No, not really."

Rising from her seat, Courtney walked to the closet. She'd made one in memory of Steven and showed it to Roger. It was in a 12" x 16" gold frame with pictures of Steven from age ten to his last visit to see Courtney. "This is the last one that I made. What do you think?"

"Wow, that's the neatest thing I've ever seen. You're very special."

"Thank you. Do you really like it?"

"Yes, I do. Could you make one for my mother with all of her children in it?"

"Sure, that would be a wonderful gift for her. Maybe when I feel better you can help me do my picture room."

Placing the collage of Steven on the baby's dresser, Roger gave Courtney a passionate kiss. He would be her baby's daddy, but Lil' Roger would also know about his biological father.

Majesta and Ah'Shiyah sat on the sofa watching television. Majesta was so tired of being alone. Most of the guys that she met were losers.

Nelson hadn't called her in months. He had never even seen Ah'Shiyah. She should have left him when she first found out what he'd done to her sister. *I wonder what Courtney's doing?*

Without giving it a second thought, she picked up the telephone and dialed Courtney's number.

"Hello."

"Hi, Roger, is Courtney busy?"

"No, she's not doing too much. She said the stitches are killing her. What are you doing?"

"We're just watching television. So how's the baby?"

"He's doing fine. He's been nursing every two hours, sometime less."

"Do you need me to come over and cook something or maybe I could go get something for you all to eat?"

"No, that's all right. Don't bring Ah'Shiyah out this time of night. Come by tomorrow. I need to run some errands; that way Courtney won't be alone. She acts like she can't be alone with the baby."

Majesta asked, "Can I talk to Courtney for a few minutes?"

"Sure, hold on."

Courtney came on the line and they talked for about thirty minutes. Majesta talked about her trip to Miami and her plans to move back home in a couple of weeks.

Chapter ten

Alex was in his last year of college. He was majoring in education because he wanted to become a teacher. Since his return from Belize, he'd changed for the best. He wasn't the player he once had been.

He was older and wise now. His player days were over. From now on he'd only sleep with women he was serious about; no more first-date sex for him.

The first woman he wanted to look up was Courtney. He'd run into Kim again and she'd told him about Courtney getting married. Alex wasn't happy to hear that news.

He regretted how he'd dropped her. It was wrong to throw three years down the drain all because of lust. He really hadn't loved Leah; she was just a sex toy. Courtney loved him and he knew it. Something in his heart told him that she still loved him.

Alex had seen Majesta in a club last night. It was her second night back and she wanted to get out and unwind. They'd danced, and he'd bought her a drink. Majesta said, "Courtney is really in love with this guy named Roger. She's in law school right now, and they're planning to get married in about a year." Alex just listened to her speak. He wanted to know all he could about Courtney's life.

"Anyway," Majesta continued, "Nelson is a jerk. I'm going to sue him for child support."

Alex couldn't believe Majesta let Nelson get her pregnant. He was sure that her baby had brothers and sisters. He'd just seen Nelson at a club about a month ago with some pregnant girl hanging on him.

Right now wasn't the time to tell Majesta about that though. She probably didn't need to hear it anyway.

Majesta said, "Courtney is coming down when her baby turn two months old."

"Really? Maybe I'll get to see her."

Majesta gave Alex her telephone number and said, "Give me a call."

Taking the number, he planned on calling her. She was his only connection to Courtney.

Alex removed the number from his dresser and called Majesta. She was staying with her mother until she and Ah'Shiyah found a place. Majesta had dropped out of college, planning to return later.

She was preparing Ah'Shiyah a bottle when the telephone rang.

"Hi, Majesta, would you like to go see a movie?" Alex asked.

"Yes, that sounds good."

"All right. I'll be over to pick you up around seven this evening."

"Okay, I'll be ready."

"Do you have any idea what you'd like to see?"

"No, I don't know what's showing. I'll let you decide if you don't mind."

"I'll look in the newspaper, and we can discuss it when I pick you up later."

Majesta hung up the telephone. She told her parents about her plans, but she didn't tell them who she was going out with.

Mr. Charles was in his wheelchair watching television like always. He did the same thing day in and day out. Every once in a while he would get depressed about being disabled. Jessica and the girls came by to keep him company. They had just left right before Alex called.

Majesta was so glad that she still had larger breasts because of her pregnancy. She could wear something revealing. Laying out a short denim skirt with a low cut body shirt, she admired her selection. Majesta completed the outfit with a new pair of brown leather sandals.

With her hair cut to her shoulders, she was wearing it straight. No one could put make-up on better than Majesta. All that modeling was paying off. She received compliments on her make-up and hair all the time. But Kim was the reason that her hair looked good. Kim didn't charge any of her sisters for doing their hair.

Majesta knew that her parents wouldn't approve of her going out with Courtney's ex-boyfriend. They knew what he'd done to their daughter was wrong. *Beggars can't be choosers. Most of the guys that I meet are married, cheating, or gay and loving it, or just prefer white women. Courtney's got a man and I plan to get one, too, even if it's her ex.*

Alex arrived on time, looking good dressed in all black. Mrs. Charles answered the door and almost closed it in his face when she saw him. She would never forget the guy who broke her daughter's heart. *What is Majesta up to?*

"Hi, Alex. So you're the mystery date."

"Hi, Mrs. Charles, it's good to see you. How's Mr. Charles?"

"He's asleep, and I don't plan on waking him either. I don't know what he would think about this surprise. Majesta is always doing things out of the norm."

"Mrs. Charles, I've changed. I don't plan on hurting any of your daughters or any other woman ever again."

"Umm huh, I've heard it all before," she replied, staring him up and down. "Have a seat, Alex. Majesta will be out soon," she replied, leaving the room.

"But, Mrs. Charles…"

Placing her hand in his face, Mrs. Charles said, "Save it. Majesta will be out in a second."

Alex sighed, and took a seat. There wasn't any point in wasting his breath. He'd have to prove himself by his actions and not his words.

Majesta finally came out five minutes later holding a sleeping baby. Alex looked at the child and commented, "She's beautiful."

"Thank you, she's precious," Majesta replied, returning the baby to the bedroom. She laid Ah'Shiyah in the crib, placing a kiss on her head.

They went to the Star Theater in the mall. Alex held her hand throughout most of the film. Majesta could feel the attraction for him. *I hope he feels it, too.*

After the romantic movie, Alex invited her to his place. When they walked in the living room, Majesta stood at the door. It was dark and she didn't want to trip over anything. Alex walked over to a lamp and turned it on. Majesta was surprised to see a neat apartment.

Taking her by the hand, Alex escorted her to the sofa. She sat down and he asked, "Would you like something to drink?"

"No, thanks."

Alex sat down beside her. Majesta inhaled the scent of him. She longed to kiss his full lips. He still had that intriguing Belize accent. They talked for what seemed like hours about everything and everybody.

Like always, Majesta gave him the low down on Courtney and her current life. She could see that Alex was interested. That's why he invited her out.

"So Majesta, you said Courtney is a mother and getting married to the father of her baby."

"No, Roger's not the baby's real father. The father died in a car accident when she was six months pregnant. She's marrying another guy. It's a long story, Alex. I'll tell you more later."

"So why did you and Nelson break up?"

"Back to Courtney again. Nelson raped her."

"Are you serious?"

"Yeah, I didn't believe it until he admitted it to me one time while he was drunk. I still tried to make it work for the baby's sake, but he ended up leaving me anyway," she stated, pausing to gather her thoughts.

"Anyway, Courtney and I fell out over the rape. I almost hated her for being with my man. She even got pregnant from him, but she got rid of it. Now my baby's daddy name is mud around my family's house while Courtney's baby's daddy is a saint. I have to admit, he really was a good guy. Now she's found someone who looks like him and acts like him. They could almost be brothers."

"You know, Majesta, I have something to tell you. I wanted to tell you this before, but I wasn't sure if I should."

"What? Just spit it out."

"I saw Nelson at a club off of Dixie Highway. He had a pregnant girl with him. Now I'm not saying it's his baby. I just know that they were together."

"I'm happy to know that he's in Miami. I already knew he was a player. I don't care who he's with; he raped my sister and left me alone to raise our child."

"So what happened to Nelson for raping Courtney?"

"Nothing. Courtney kept it a secret for a while. Then, one day she told Kim and Jessica. I found out last year, almost three years after the rape. Nelson was the only one for me. He could do no wrong. Everybody tried to tell me that he was no good. I just didn't listen."

Alex fought internally to control his anger. He couldn't believe that Nelson put his hands on Courtney and no one had done anything to him. If he could get his hands on Nelson, he'd kick his natural born butt.

Majesta could tell that Alex still had feeling for Courtney. It seemed like the whole conversation revolved around her. She was tired of talking. She was ready to make out or go home.

"Alex, are you still in love with my sister?"

"I do care about your sister. I guess I always will."

"I'm tired of short term relationships. I want a man that cares for me and my baby, too. We're a packaged deal."

"I understand what you're saying, Majesta. I'm not looking for a relationship right now."

"It seems every guy that I want, wants Courtney. I loved Nelson so much. He was my first love. But he wanted Courtney, so he raped her. Then I met Roger at church. His sister introduced me to him, and I really liked him. Courtney came down later, and he flipped over her. Now you're trying to get her, too, Alex."

"Majesta, I like you. Before we get sexually involved, I have to love you. I never planned on scoring with you. Now I can't say what I would do if you pushed me. I would love to get to know you and your baby though."

"Thanks for your honesty. It's appreciated."

Majesta relaxed. She and Alex continued talking until morning.

"You're welcome to sleep on my sofa."

"No, I need to get back to my baby."

He liked that she was being a responsible mother. Alex drove Majesta to her parents' house before daybreak and walked her to the door like a gentleman.

Leaning over, he captured Majesta's lips into a passionate kiss. Majesta felt a chill run all over her body.

"Would you and Ah'Shiyah have dinner with me later this evening?"

"Yes, I like that you included my baby."

Alex was indeed a changed man. She couldn't wait to tell Kim and Jessica about the new and improved Alex.

Driving back home, Alex felt confused. His heart still wanted Courtney, but his body was feeling Majesta. And since they were both single, he figured it wouldn't hurt to get to know this lady better. *If Courtney has moved on with her new man, what else can I do?*

Chapter eleven

Mariah was adjusting to her father being out of the house. She didn't like it when her mama had that man in their house. He was always coming around and staying in her mom's room. She told Paul, "My daddy is going to be back, and he's going to beat you up." Then she kicked him, stuck out her tongue, and ran to her room.

He didn't bother mentioning this incident to Jessica. He knew that the child was only acting out because she missed her father.

Paul was good to Jessica. Besides that, he made her feel sexy. Thanks to him she'd lost forty pounds with thirty to go. He introduced her to a great fat free, water drinking life. Jessica also stopped eating after seven o'clock in the evening.

She and William were acting civil for the kids' sake. It looked like the divorce would be final in a month. Jessica would get the house, the van, and most of the things in the house. All he wanted were his personal belongings.

William admitted that he couldn't take care of the girls like Jessica. He was pleased with the way that she kept them dressed, their hair was always combed, and their hygiene up to par.

Jessica still loved William, and she believed that he loved her. William came over while the girls were at Jessica's parents' house. Jessica had on a tight black body dress showing off her new shape.

She and Paul had planned an evening together at his place. Jessica was in the kitchen cooking their dinner when the door bell rang. When she opened it, William looked at her like he didn't recognize her.

Fixing her dress, Jessica smiled at him and said, "Hi, William."

"Jessica, you look great," he commented, admiring her from head to toe.

"Thank you."

"Where did you get that body?"

"I had it on layaway, and I just got it out," she replied. William hadn't seen much of Jessie lately. She dropped the girls off at her parents' house so that he could pick them up and return them there without seeing her. So he didn't have any idea how much weight his wife had actually lost.

Smiling, William walked in the house. Jessica went back in the kitchen to check on the low fat meal that she was preparing. William followed her and sat at the kitchen table.

"I hope you keep the weight off."

"I will. I love my new shape. I will not give in to the fat life again."

William didn't say anything in response to that remark. He just watched Jessica cook her special shrimp fried rice. "I've been cooking lots of low fat meals."

"That's good. Jessie, where are the things that I left here?"

"Whatever you left is in the study in a box with your name on it."

He got up from the table, went to the study, and found the box in a corner. Then he placed the box at the front door and walked around the house.

William entered Mariah and Jasmine's room. It was clean and everything was in its proper place. There was a collage that their Aunt Courtney had made for them a couple of years ago. It was in a 14" x 16" inch pink frame. *What a neat piece of art work.*

Regretting moving out, William realized how much he missed his home, his girls, and even his wife. *I hate the one bedroom apartment I'm living in. It's so dull and sad.*

He thought that he wanted freedom, but Jessica had already given him all the freedom he needed. She'd always taken care of the girls and never nagged or questioned him. *I didn't know how good I had it.*

Even now, Jessica wasn't nagging him about anything. She went on with her life like she really didn't care about him anymore. It was tearing him apart.

Jessica didn't need his money. Her dad was rich.

I wonder why her parents never moved out of their house when they got all that money from the settlement. They just fixed the house up and added a new room with a swimming pool. And they changed the house to meet Mr. Charles' handicapped needs but that's it.

Jessica shared closeness with her family that William didn't have with his. It's no wonder she was adjusting so well. *I wonder about this new man in her life. I don't want another man in my daughters' lives. I'm all the daddy they need.*

William ended up back in the kitchen. Jessica was placing the dinner in the oven to keep warm until she was ready to leave.

She placed a vegetable platter in the refrigerator next to a fruit platter filled with extra pineapples and strawberries. Paul was providing the drinks and entertainment for the evening. Dinner was set for six o'clock.

Glancing at her watch, Jessica noted that it was two hours before she'd have to leave. She was very timely. It would only take thirty minutes to get to Paul's place in Kendall. But she planned to leave at five so that she'd have plenty of time to get through traffic.

"Boy, that smells good, Jessie Poo."

William hadn't called her that in years. She knew that he was up to something. "I have dinner plans later. You're welcome to take a plate with you when you leave."

"Thank you, I'll do that."

Taking off her apron, Jessica revealed more of her shape. William gave her a seductive look and walked over to where she stood. Jessica was surprised to see him coming on to her. She hated herself for liking it, but Jessie couldn't control the attraction to her husband. This was a man that knew every part of her anatomy and how to work it.

William placed his hands on her hips, and then he pulled her close to his torso. The way he looked at her, she knew that he wanted to be intimate once more.

He thought about his relationship with Sandra and how good she was in bed or anywhere he wanted it. They'd done it in the car, his office, outside on the patio, on the beach under the stars, in the tub, and in the shower. She was a freak. But Jessica was a decent woman and that's what he wanted now.

They made hot passionate love on the kitchen floor. Jessica couldn't get enough of his heated touches. Even though Paul had been spending some nights with her, she still missed William's special brand of loving.

When the cooking was done between Jessica and William, they remained on the floor talking. They talked about the kids and the pending divorce.

It wasn't long before they were hungry. The naked Jessica washed her hands and fixed two plates of food.

She spread a sheet across the kitchen floor, got a bottle of wine, and poured two glasses of it. Then they fed each other in the nude, loving every moment of it.

Jessica couldn't ever remember having such a romantic evening with her husband. Suddenly, she remembered Paul.

Rushing to the telephone in her bedroom, Jessica made a quick call to Paul. She said, "Hi, Paul. I'm not going to be able to make it tonight. My cycle just came on, and I'm feeling terrible."

"I was really looking forward to seeing you, Jessie."

"I know, but we'll do it another time. I have to go take some Midol or something."

"Okay, I'll come by tomorrow to check on you."

Jessica hung up the telephone, returned to the kitchen, and placed the dirty plates in the sink. She took the wine and the glasses to the bedroom while William followed close behind.

Getting into bed, they snuggled up just like a real husband and wife. Before day the next morning, they woke up and made love again.

Chapter twelve

Mrs. Williams was in the kitchen cooking dinner for Roger, Courtney, and Lil' Roger, who were on their way over. She was so proud of her son, and she was looking forward to spending time with Courtney and Lil' Roger.

Thinking of her past, Mrs. Williams remembered her high school days. Teresa had been forced to deal with the embarrassment of being a single expectant mother. She dropped out of school and never returned to get her diploma. It had always hurt her that she dropped out in her senior year.

When she met her late husband, Roger was two-years-old. Thinking about it, Roger was a lot like Sherman Williams, III. Roger loved him so much. He didn't believe it when she first told him that Sherman wasn't his real father.

Roger tried so hard to be like Sherman. *Courtney's baby will think the same thing about him, but there isn't a real father to show her baby. Roger's father is out there somewhere. Maybe one day he'll find him. I wonder if he ever got married or had any other children.*

The door bell rang, and she opened it to see Roger holding the baby and Courtney holding the baby bag. Courtney had lost a lot of weight. She and the baby were getting ready to go visit the baby's grandfather. He was very anxious to see his only grandchild from what she'd heard.

"Thanks for coming over to dinner. I wanted to see you and Lil' Roger before you all left," she said, reaching for the baby.

"Thanks for having us over, Mrs. Williams. We're always happy to visit with you."

"What time are you all leaving tomorrow?"

"Our flight leaves at 1:15 p.m."

Mrs. Williams just couldn't get over how much the baby favored Roger when he was a baby. "What are you feeding this child? He's just as big as you and Courtney."

They all laughed together.

"Roger, you were big just like this child at this age," she said. Turning towards Courtney, she continued, "He was the biggest baby I ever had. He came in this world weighing nine pounds and five ounces. His other brothers and sisters didn't weigh over eight pounds when they were born."

She went and got a picture of Roger to show Courtney how much the baby resembled him. Courtney said, "Boy, it's true. Everyone does have a twin."

"I told you that he looked like me."

"Yes, you did."

They enjoyed looking at the old photograph of Roger while Mrs. Williams played with the baby. "So, Courtney, are you ready for your trip?"

"Not really. I'm really not in the mood for traveling. I'm just going because I promised that I would." Courtney had been fighting depression lately. She hadn't eaten much in weeks. She'd stopped breast feeding because her milk was getting low. And she hadn't done much with the baby or for the baby. Roger was doing just about everything.

Mrs. Williams asked, "What's Lil' Roger's grandfather's name? I might know him."

As Courtney began to speak, the telephone rang. Mrs. Williams said, "Excuse me for just a second, please."

Her daughter, Maggie, was on the line. She was sick with the flu, and needed her mother to come get her daughter, Tabatha.

Grabbing her purse and keys, Mrs. Williams said, "You all help yourselves to dinner. I don't know when I'll be back."

She hugged Courtney and Lil' Roger. They said their goodbyes and Mrs. Williams left.

Courtney said, "I'm not real hungry. Can we just fix a plate and take it home?"

"Sure, that'll work," Roger replied.

Before leaving, they looked at Roger's photo album that Mrs. Williams had pulled out. It was neatly put together. She had pictures of herself from when she was pregnant with Roger, pictures of him as a newborn, and recent ones. He was the only one of her children with a special photo album.

Courtney said, "I can see that you and your mother have a very special relationship."

"Yeah, I guess we do."

They fixed their food and headed home. Courtney was tired. She needed to rest. Weeks had passed since she'd had a good night's sleep.

It wasn't Lil' Roger that was keeping her from resting; it was her bad thoughts and dreams. Courtney was afraid that she was going to harm her baby for some reason. That's why she hadn't been alone with him in the last three weeks.

Courtney got an awful feeling in the pit of her stomach every time she was with her baby. She told Roger that she was sick so that he would start taking care of the baby more.

I love my baby. Why am I afraid of hurting him? Maybe it's time for me to go back to counseling. Maybe I need to get some medication. There has to be some type of explainable reason for what I'm feeling.

I need to talk with Roger. I don't know about traveling alone with the baby right now.

Sitting on the side of the bed, Courtney contemplated how she was going to explain her dilemma to Roger. *He might leave me if he knows what I'm thinking. Oh, God, what am I going to do?*

"Roger, come here, please. I need to talk."

"What's wrong, baby? Why are you crying? Are you sick?"

"Yes, I'm depressed."

"What do you mean?"

Being a God-fearing Christian, Roger remained calm while Courtney explained her situation. He had already heard about her mental problems from his sister. His love was strong for her. He was prepared to handle anything that she had to say.

"If I tell you this, will you still be here for me?"

"You can tell me anything. I'm not going anywhere."

"I need you more now than I did when Lil' Roger was born. This pain is worse than labor itself. I can't find peace of mind. Evil thoughts are coming from everywhere. Why did they start and why won't they stop?"

Staring at the palms of her hands, Courtney continued talking as he took one of her hands and held it. "Talk to me," he begged. "Tell me what's bothering you. Why don't you take care of Lil' Roger anymore? And what do you mean you're mentally ill?"

"I've had mental problems in the past. I've been trying to cope with them for years, but I can't handle this. I need help. I need rest and peace of mind."

Courtney took her time telling Roger about her OCD. She explained how she'd taken medications off and on to control her obsessive behavior. "It's never bothered people around me. They just think that I'm clean and orderly."

"I see."

"I check things, Roger. I have to keep checking the doors, appliances, and windows over and over again. And I'm so afraid of germs that I use too much bleach to clean the house."

Swallowing her pride, Courtney continued speaking. "I've lightened up when it comes to sex. It doesn't really bother me anymore. At first, I couldn't stand anyone sweating on me or kissing me. But I thought that I was getting better. Now I'm having some really crazy thoughts night and day."

"What do you think about?"

"I dreamed that I did something awful to Lil' Roger. And sometime thoughts come to me to drown him, drop him, or burn him. I only have dreams of hurting him, but not you or any other person, just him, just my baby."

Roger listened to her in silence. He felt sorry for Courtney as the tears ran like a waterfall from her eyes. She had broken out in hives all over her chest and face. Her ears were red. She looked so feeble, so harmless.

"You could never hurt anyone, better yet Lil' Roger. You love your baby. Besides, I won't let you hurt him, okay? I'll watch over him and you."

She continued crying as he tried comforting her. But nothing he said would stop her tears.

I've seen her cutting out pictures of the baby. She was making a collage for him. I've been looking for it, but I can't find it. She must have hidden it somewhere. Could this be the blues that some women get after childbirth? She's not up to traveling anywhere.

"You are too sweet of a person to hurt anyone," he reassured her. "We're going to fix this problem. You'll see."

"Roger, I love my baby, and I want to do motherly things for him. I wish I could just nurse him again, change him, give him a bath, or just hold him, but I'm afraid."

"I think that you should cancel the trip. You can get a refund or change it to another day."

"Roger, Dr. Palmer is looking forward to seeing his grandson. This is his only grandchild."

"It doesn't matter. Your health is more important to me."

Roger got Lil' Roger out of his crib. He carried the baby to Courtney. "Here, hold your baby. I'll sit right by you."

He handed the sleeping infant to her. Courtney held him very carefully as if it was her first time.

Placing her face next to his soft face, she kissed his sweet smelling head. As she held him, tears filled her puffy eyes again.

Courtney handed Lil' Roger back to Roger who laid him in the crib. She reached for her purse, pulled out the airline tickets, and rescheduled for another date. "I'm not sure I'll be able to travel," she told the agent.

The receptionist said, "We can reschedule for thirty days from today. If you change your mind, you can always call us back."

"Thanks, I really appreciate that."

Courtney looked drained. Roger told her, "You should go to bed."

Following his advice, she changed into her nightgown and climbed into bed. Since Roger wasn't sleepy, he took the baby into the living with him to watch television.

Courtney tried her hardest to go to sleep, but she only tossed and turned. She just felt awful.

Lying there with her eyes closed, she called on the Lord. "Dear God, please hear my prayer. Give me peace, dear Lord. Fix my mind that I may never have thoughts to harm anyone. Give me the mind of Christ. Please be with me, dear Lord. Let me know that you are there. Bless my child. Bless Roger. You are the only one that can help me, God. Please, it's in Jesus name that I pray. Amen."

Courtney forced herself to think about a happy time in her life, a time when she was doing okay mentally. She was a little girl sitting on the porch. It was early in the morning and everyone was still in bed. She sat on the porch on that overcast morning thinking about Jacob's ladder.

She imagined a ladder going straight to heaven. Courtney remembered feeling happy that morning. Her faith in God was strong and personal then.

Longing for that type of relationship again, she wanted to be like a child in her heart, that childlike feeling about God. Courtney prayed for that feeling.

She liked herself then, but she had changed through the years. *How wonderful a child like spirit would be.*

Finally, calmness came over her. Before she knew it, Courtney was in a dream.

Chapter thirteen

Kim heard about Majesta's new man and she couldn't believe who it was. When Jessica told her that Majesta had gone out with Courtney's first love, the guy that broke her heart, Kim just couldn't believe it. Why would she date someone that had broken her sister's heart?

Everybody knows that Alex is Courtney's heart no matter what he's done in the past. If Courtney knew that Majesta was dating him, she would really lose her mind.

"I think they're getting serious," Jessica told Kim. "They came over to the house several times hugging and holding hands."

"That's ludicrous."

Kim and Jessica talked about Majesta everyday regarding her selfish behavior. Kim told Majesta on the telephone, "You're not welcome to bring Alex to my house."

She thought about Jessica and how she'd easily given in to William. *Will my sisters ever get their love lives together?*

Kim didn't believe that Courtney was in love with Roger. To her, it was just a rebound relationship.

Courtney had been with Alex longer than Attorney Parker, Steven, or Roger. I'm glad that she took my advice and is waiting before marrying Roger. If he loves her like he claims he does, he'll wait.

Kim was concerned about Courtney. Every time that she called her, Courtney's voice sounded shaky. And they wouldn't talk for very long anymore.

Courtney had promised to bring the baby so that they could see him. Kim already had many pictures of Lil' Roger, and judging from them, she was amazed at how much the baby actually favored Roger. He even had his nose and those dark thick eyebrows.

While Kim was in deep thought, Carlton, Jr. walked in the kitchen to show her a poem he'd written. Kim read the poem out loud. It was titled, "Think How The World Would Be If There Wasn't the Black Race."

She read,

"Think how the world would be, if there wasn't the black race.

There would be no strength, for we are a strong race.

There would be no compassion, for we are a compassionate race.

There would be no beauty, for we are a colorful and beautiful race.

It's hard to imagine a world without my people.

The race all others came from.

Black children, be proud of your black race.

Show strength by overcoming the temptations of drugs and material things.

Strengthen your hearts and minds with the Word of God.

For one day, our children will become the leaders of the world again.

We are compassionate, and we will be just.

Express your inner and outer beauty, the world is watching.

Sing black people because the world loves your songs.

Don't let the world tell you what you're not, for we are the race who gave the world what it's got."

Kim was so proud of her oldest child. He was smarter than any fourth grader, even after skipping the third grade. "Did your daddy help you?" Kim asked.

"No, mama, these are my thoughts. I'm going to be a famous author one day. I've been working on a book."

Kim wasn't surprised because he was gifted from birth. She put an "A" on the paper and gave him a hug.

Kim walked to her room and got changed for work. She was getting tired of doing hair and nails. It was something that she'd been doing all of her life. Being the oldest of four girls, she practiced on her sisters, who all had long thick wavy hair. Carlton had already told Kim that she could stop working whenever she was ready, but she enjoyed having her separate spending money.

Carlton paid the bills out of his earnings which left Kim with plenty of funds for the mall, her second home. Her shop was in the mall, and when she wasn't working, she was shopping at the most expensive stores they had.

She and her sisters believed in dressing their children well, too. Her boys had wall to wall clothes and shoes in their walk-in closet. She also shopped for her nieces and nephew.

The twins entered the room, speaking at the same time like they usually did. "Mama, can we have some cookies, please?"

"No, did you two pick up your toys and make up those beds?"

"We're still playing," they replied together.

"Where is Jeremy? He's mighty quiet."

"He's in Carlton's room sleeping."

Jeremy loved to be around his big brother. Kim went to the room and found her baby sleeping in Carlton's bed. She often took Jeremy over to Jessica's so that he could play with Jasmine. They got along very well.

Closing the door, Kim told Carlton, Jr., "Watch out for your brothers. Give Jeremy a peanut butter sandwich and milk when he gets up." The twins had already eaten.

Kim walked to her room to find Carlton, Sr. still sleeping, too. This was his day off and he needed the rest.

They hardly went anywhere lately. Kim found herself mostly in the shop while Carlton was at the office. They wanted to take a cruise over the summer, leaving the boys with her parents.

She and Carlton only had sex about four times a month and sometimes less than that. It just wasn't a big deal to her anymore.

They both worked long hours. All they wanted when they got home was a good night's sleep.

Backing out of the room, she closed the door, thinking, *I've got to get to work. It's Saturday and it's going to be busy.*

Chapter fourteen

Thanks for tuning in. This is Live With Dhawana Rivers with the five o'clock news. Today, a southside woman killed her five-month-old baby boy. She had a history of mental illness. Her friends reported that they couldn't believe it. 'Courtney wouldn't hurt a flea,' they said.

Waking up with her body covered in sweat, Courtney could barely breathe. This was the worst of all of her dreams. She saw blood everywhere. It seemed so real.

Roger was still sleeping with Lil' Roger cradled next to him. Courtney got out of the bed and changed her gown. She was so bony; her breasts looked out of place. They seemed too heavy for her to carry. She'd often wished that she could have them reduced.

Courtney looked in the mirror; she could see her pelvic bone poking out. This was the worst that she'd ever looked in her life. The dream had shaken her up so bad that she couldn't even look at the baby.

Walking by Roger, she went to the guest bedroom with a bad feeling in the pit of her stomach. "Please, Lord, help me. Make it stop. I don't wanna to hurt my baby," she prayed.

Roger woke up to find Courtney gone. He panicked remembering what she'd told him. He didn't know what to do. *She might be suicidal. I know she's starving herself to death. She looks like skin and bones.*

Placing Lil' Roger in his crib, he went looking for Courtney. He found her in the guest room lying on the floor, shaking with fear. "Courtney, what's wrong?"

"I had a bad dream about the baby. Blood was everywhere. It was horrible."

"Lil' Roger is all right. I just put him in his crib. Let's go see him. Come on, Courtney."

Courtney eased up. Roger held her hand, walking her to Lil' Roger's crib. He was lying on his back sucking his fist.

Roger picked the baby up and handed him to Courtney. She acted as if she didn't want to hold him or even knew how. Roger could see that she wasn't in any condition to be holding a baby so he said, "Okay, let me have him back now. He's fine."

Placing the baby in the crib, Roger turned to Courtney. "You need to eat something before you starve to death."

"I might be able to eat something today."

"Get back in bed. I'm going to fix you some hot cereal," Roger said, leaving for the kitchen with the baby carrier in his hand. "I'm going to make him a bottle and get you some breakfast."

Courtney was weak. She didn't know which way to turn. She needed peace, somewhere all by herself. Roger had done so much for her already from changing to feeding the baby; he did everything a mother would do. He even took Lil' Roger to his mother's house when he went to school.

Roger had talked to Kim and Jessica about Courtney's deteriorating condition. They were planning to come visit them the following weekend but he needed to do something for Courtney now. His woman needed help, and she needed it today.

Entering the room with a bowl of hot cereal in his hand, Roger was hurting to see Courtney this miserable. *She was excited about the baby when she was pregnant. She even made me excited about it, too. I can't believe this is the same woman that I met at church. She was happy then. She took care of herself. She was well groomed. Now I have to tell her to take baths, comb her hair, and brush her teeth. Courtney used to be clean. She didn't let her apartment get dusty like it is now.*

Roger tried his best to keep the place in order like the old Courtney did. He knew this was something serious. Roger had faith that God would heal Courtncy. God would show him the way.

He made up his mind that he was going to get Courtney some help that very day.

"Honey, let's eat."

Courtney started shaking her head as soon as she saw the bowl. Seriously depressed, she wanted peace of mind and not food.

"Courtney, just eat a little, okay."

Placing the spoon to her mouth, Roger wished that she would at least try to eat a bite. She took in a little bit, but then she let it fall right out of her mouth.

Taking a napkin, he wiped her face. He then laid her down and covered her with a sheet.

Lil' Roger had fallen asleep in his carrier. Roger took him out, placing him back in the bed. He felt sorry for Lil' Roger, too. His father was dead, and his mother was afraid that she was going to kill him. Now Roger felt like a mother and father at the same time.

He adored Lil' Roger, but he was ready for a break. He couldn't wait for Kim and Jessica to come take care of the baby for a little while. Lil' Roger was a good boy. He just seemed to stay up when Roger was studying or trying to get some sleep. But the two of them had bonded. The baby cried every time Roger dropped him off at his mother's house.

I should have married Courtney, at least for the baby's sake. What if she doesn't get better and her family come and take Lil' Roger? Oh, God help us.

Roger got dressed in jeans and a black shirt, called his mom, and asked, "Can you watch Lil' Roger for a while?"

"Sure, bring him on over."

"How's Maggie? Is she over the flu yet?"

"Your sister's fine. I have to run an errand. I'll just take the baby with me."

"All right."

"Just bring his stroller. If you want me to keep him overnight, bring enough Pampers and formula."

"Thank you, mama, you're the greatest. We'll come back in a few hours. There will be cereal in each bottle to keep him full."

He got the baby's stroller out of the closet, placing it next to the door. Roger knew what had to be done. Courtney needed to be in a hospital; she was starving herself to death.

Roger had shared Courtney's behavior with his mother. "I've never heard of such a thing before," she replied.

After preparing a bath, Roger picked up Courtney and placed her in the tub. He brushed her teeth right there in the tub, and she spit in the water.

The only thing he had a problem with was combing all of her hair. He got a brush and a hair clip and brushed her hair back into a ponytail. Then he bathed her from head to toe.

Helping her stand up, Roger dried off Courtney's body then dressed her in jeans and a t-shirt with socks and her running shoes. As he dressed her, she didn't utter a word.

They dropped off Lil' Roger and headed to the closest hospital's mental ward. Since it was obvious that Courtney was in a bad state of mind, the nurse checked her in right away.

Courtney signed the admission papers and started crying uncontrollably. Roger had never seen her crying like this. *I wonder how her family is going to react to all of this. Her parents might want her to come back to Miami. I just hope that it doesn't come to that.*

He only wanted the love of his life to get better. This was the only thing left for him to do. If he had waited another day, she might have died.

The nurse weighed Courtney. She was only ninety-four pounds. Being five feet six, she looked like a skeleton.

Shaking her head, Courtney stepped off of the scale. The nurse inserted an intravenous feeding tube into her right arm before administering medications to help her rest.

It was morning when Courtney finally woke up. Looking around the room, she wondered why she let Roger bring her to this place. The screaming, laughing, and loud talking was scaring her.

A nurse entered the room and asked, "I see you're awake. Are you hungry?"

"No, I'm not."

"There will be a doctor coming in to ask you some questions."

"Can you take this tube out of my arm? I want to go home."

"If you want the tube out, you have to eat. When you talk to the doctor, she will decide if you are mentally ready to leave.

"I'm not crazy. I'm just really sad."

"The doctor will be in shortly."

Soon, Dr. Simon, a petite female, came in. She appeared to be in her fifties with salt and pepper hair. Courtney sat up in the bed, trying to straighten her gown.

"Hello, Ms. Charles. I understand that you voluntarily admitted yourself to this hospital."

"Yes."

"You have a history of OCD and you're showing signs of depression."

"I'm just sad."

"Okay, Courtney, why are you sad?"

Tears welled up in her eyes as she told the doctor about her dreams and evil thoughts. She told the doctor, "My baby's father died in a car wreck while I was pregnant. I miss him a lot. Now I'm afraid I'm going to kill my baby. I just wish that these thoughts would go away. I want to take care of my child, but I'm afraid to be alone with him. I can't understand why these bad things are happening to me."

"Courtney, it's common for some women to suffer these emotions after a pregnancy. It's called post partum depression. We're going to keep you here in the Psychiatric Unit for further evaluations. Hopefully, after a week of rest along with proper medication, you'll be able to get back to a normal life."

A week or two away from the outside world sounded great to Courtney. She was desperate.

Once the doctor left, someone came in and took a picture of Courtney for their records. Another young nurse came in and helped her take a shower, wash her hair, comb it up into a ponytail, and change into a clean gown.

About an hour later, Courtney was done. She returned to sat on the freshly made up bed. The medications were already starting to work. Not once did she have a bad thought.

Courtney was feeling better; she even had an appetite now. She called the nurse's station, asking someone to bring her in a tray of food.

After Courtney completed her first solid meal, the nurse removed the IV. And it felt great to finally have the intravenous feeding tube out of her arm.

Dr. Simon knocked on the door and asked, "Would you like to sit in the recreation area?"

"Yes, I'll try."

There were tables, chairs, books, games, a television, a snack machine, and a puzzle table in the recreation center. It was a terrific place to relax. When Courtney saw the puzzle, she thought about her collages. *That's all my collages are, pictures neatly cut and arranged carefully in a picture frame, like pieces of a puzzle.*

Courtney saw people from every race in this area. There were African-Americans, Caucasians, Mexicans, Asian, and Native Americans. There were young, middle aged, and elderly people participating in activities.

The doctor sat Courtney next to a window overlooking a picnic area with chairs, tables, and benches. They talked about everything. Courtney really opened up to Dr. Simon, telling her about her family, her love life, and her OCD history. She even told the doctor about how she was raped by her sister's boyfriend. "I didn't report it because I thought that it was all my fault."

"Unfortunately, that's usually what happens," the doctor responded, writing down everything.

Then Courtney told her about Steven and his sudden death. "I feel like I let him down by not taking care of his baby," she said, remembering him.

Then the memory of the bad dreams and evil thoughts came rushing back. She felt the tears welling up in her eyes again.

Wiping her face and running nose with a Kleenex tissue, Courtney watched the doctor continue writing. "I feel love in my heart for my baby. It's my brain that tells me to do bad things to him. Please, doctor, make it stop. I want to raise my son. I don't want to depend on my family or Roger to do that."

"Things will get better for you if you continue taking your medication. You're just tired and depressed. We're going to start you on a different prescription. You'll be feeling better within a week."

That night, Courtney slept really well. Her roommate, Amanda, was there for beating up an elderly relative. She was also beaten up. Her eyes were swollen shut. Amanda wasn't able to see, but she was definitely able to talk. And that night, she talked Courtney to sleep.

At six o'clock the next morning, the nurse woke them up for their medications. Courtney went to the bathroom, brushed her teeth, and washed her face. She slicked her hair back by wetting the hairbrush.

Courtney got in line to receive her medication. She couldn't believe how much she wanted it.

Amanda said, "You're not crazy. Why are you here?"

"I'm depressed. I'm afraid to be alone with my baby. I've had thoughts of harming him."

"Are you married or a single mother like me? Evan and me don't have nobody. He's in foster care, but I'm going to get my baby back one day."

"I'm not married. My baby's daddy died when I was pregnant. My fiancé, Roger, is taking care of him while I'm here. He's been with us since my pregnancy. He loves me and my son."

"That's good. Somebody loves you. I don't have nobody to love me. Everybody thinks I'm violent."

"Don't worry about that, Amanda. God loves you, and He knows your heart."

Courtney was next in line to receive her medication. She took her pills, washing them down with water. Then she went back to her room, laid down in bed, and thought about Roger.

She felt like she was on a vacation. Everyone was really nice to her. Courtney even felt comfortable talking to the doctors. She'd seen at least four doctors since her arrival, and each one seemed to understand her. That alone made her feel better.

In this place, she saw people with worse problems than hers. Courtney thanked God for saving her life and for showing her that no matter where you are; someone is doing worse.

Roger had called her several times, but Courtney didn't want to see or talk to anyone. She asked the staff not to allow any visitors for her. Roger couldn't understand why Courtney wouldn't talk to him. He was deeply hurt and on top of that, her family was upset with him for taking Courtney to a mental institution without calling them first.

Roger was tired from having to take care of the baby and trying to attend law school. If it wasn't for his mother, he would have dropped out a long time ago. He could get her to watch Lil' Roger anytime.

He'd talked to Courtney's sisters from the hospital about how bad her condition was. Kim told him, "I appreciate what you've done for my nephew. But I wish you would have waited until we saw her before signing her in to a mental hospital."

Roger replied, "Courtney admitted herself. I just drove her to the hospital. I didn't think that it could wait any longer because she was having thoughts of hurting the baby."

With a worried look on his face, Roger hung up the telephone and called his mother to check on Lil' Roger. "He's doing fine. I'm glad to take care of him. Son, you did the right thing. She was so thin that she needed to be somewhere. They will take care of the physical state once they fix her mental state. Don't feel sorry for what you did. I'm proud of you. Tell Courtney's sister to call me."

After closing the conversation with his mother, Roger felt better. He knew Courtney wouldn't have let him take her to the hospital if she didn't need to go.

The next day when Kim, Jessica, and Majesta got off the airplane, Roger was there to pick them up. They gave him hugs and went by his mother's house to see Lil' Roger.

Courtney still wasn't taking calls, and she didn't want visitors but her sister's were sure she would talk to them. Courtney proved them wrong. Dr. Simon said, "Your sisters really want to see you."

Courtney replied, "I don't want them to see me in this condition. They can go see Lil' Roger so that their trip won't be in vain."

"Okay, but think about seeing them before they leave, even if it's just for a few minutes. They're your sisters. They love you no matter what."

Nodding her head in agreement, Courtney released a sigh. A couple of days later, she told Dr. Simon, "I'm ready to see my sisters."

"That's wonderful news. They'll be so happy to see you."

Courtney's sisters couldn't believe their eyes. She didn't sound like herself at all to them. This person was nonchalant, seemingly drugged. Courtney didn't even ask about the rest of the family including her parents. She only spoke when she was asked a direct question. It hurt them to hear their sister sound this strange.

Majesta said, "Alex Reyes asked about you."

Courtney didn't respond to that either.

Finally, they left in silence to go sit in the waiting area. Kim said to her sisters, "Mom and dad don't need to know about her medical condition. Dad's been real sick lately and this would kill him."

They all agreed. Jessica added, "Courtney's been suffering from OCD, and when Nelson raped her, she only went back to therapy for a short while. Maybe she can get the help that she needs in here."

Majesta shared with her sisters, "Alex and I are planning to get engaged. I think Courtney should know about it."

Kim said, "You should wait until she's mentally better. She can't handle that right now. Besides, are you sure that you're ready for this big step?"

"I know what I'm doing, Kim. I love Alex, and he loves me too."

Roger was staying with his mother so Courtney's sisters could have the whole place to themselves. He didn't want to interfere with their time together.

Jessica was in Courtney's kitchen making a chicken casserole dinner and listening to Kim talk.

Walking into the living with a scowl on her face, Jessie said, "You're dating Alex out of spite."

"Listen, I wasn't looking to fall in love with Courtney's ex-boyfriend. It just happened. I've been alone for too long. You got a husband, Kim. Jessica, you got two men in your life. Courtney got the man I wanted. Now I got the man she wanted. That's life, and I'm enjoying it."

Nothing else was said concerning Alex and Majesta. They went back to Miami and told their parents that Courtney was doing fine. "She just needs some rest," Jessie said.

Three days later, Courtney went home. She had started eating regularly and gained five pounds, but she was still underweight according to medical standards. Amanda, her roommate, still had to stay three more weeks. "I'm glad at least one of us is going home," she said as Courtney prepared to leave.

"You'll be out soon, don't worry about it."

On the day Roger picked up Courtney, they went straight home. When they entered the apartment, they could smell freshness all over it. Her sisters had dusted, vacuumed, mopped, disinfected the bathroom, washed all the dishes, and put them away. The place was spotless.

Courtney was very pleased to see her place looking normal again. She hadn't cleaned it in weeks. Roger did the best he could, but it wasn't like Courtney.

"Did my sisters do this?"

"Yes, they did. I've been at my mom's. They were here with Lil' Roger most of the time."

Roger placed Courtney's things in the bedroom.

Walking around the apartment, Courtney admired how sparkling clean it was.

Roger was pleased with Courtney's recovery. He would make sure that she took her medication on time everyday. The doctor had told him, "If she wants to get better, it's important that she takes her medication at the same time each day and there won't be a problem."

I wonder why she hasn't asked about Lil' Roger. Anyway, I'll pick him up tomorrow. If she asks me to go get him tonight, then I'll be glad to do it.

That night, Courtney wanted to make love. She took a shower, sprayed on Opium, her favorite perfume, slipped into her emerald green teddy set, and climbed into bed.

Roger walked in the room startled to see Courtney sitting up with a pillow behind her back smiling at him. He walked over to her, placing a barely there kiss on her lips. Then he took off his clothes and eased into bed beside her.

Roger tried to make it last forever. He wanted to hold back until Courtney was completely satisfied. But after thirty minutes, their loving session was ended.

Courtney had taken her medication an hour earlier and was feeling very sleepy. She was out for the remainder of the night and most of the morning.

Around noon the next day, Courtney woke up. Roger called his mom, asking her to get Lil' Roger ready for pick up.

"How is she, Roger?"

"She's fine. I think she's going to be better than ever now. The real test will come when she sees Lil' Roger. I'm not going to push her to take care of him right now."

"See you later, son."

Courtney was in the shower by the time Roger hung up the telephone. He decided that it was time for him to take one too so he stepped into the tub to join Courtney.

He came up close behind her, sharing the warm soapy suds from her body. Turning around, Courtney kissed him directly on the lips.

They felt the same arousal that they'd shared the night before. Deepening their kiss, they continued bathing each other until their bodies connected under the steaming shower head.

Once they were both satisfied, they bathed for real. Within minutes, they were both dressed in jeans and pullover shirts and on their way to retrieve their son.

Chapter fifteen

Dr. Palmer was upset that Courtney didn't make the trip. He told her, "I'll be glad to come out there to see you and the baby."

"No, no, that's okay. I've been under the weather, and that wouldn't be a good idea. I should be able to visit you within another month or so for sure."

"I don't want to wait another month. From the pictures you sent me, he looks just like Steven. I can't wait that long to hold my only grandchild in my arms."

"I understand. It's up to you."

"Courtney, I've changed my will so that Lil' Roger is the heir to my entire fortune. I wanted you to know that in case anything happens to me before I can get there."

"Don't talk like that. Nothings going to happen to you, you're not going anywhere."

"It seems that everyone that I love is dead except for my grandson and you. My wife and my son are both gone. I'm a widower with no children. But God being a merciful God has left me a grandson, and I plan to spend a lot of time with him."

"I'm looking forward to you seeing him. He's an energetic little boy."

"To be honest with you, Courtney, I've even thought about relocating to the Houston area. I could wait until all my patients have their babies, and I've stopped taking on any new patients. I might fly down there week after next to look at some office space."

"I'm happy to hear that. You'd love Houston. And it would be great to have you closer to us."

"How are things between you and the young man that you've been seeing?"

"Ah, we're doing fine. I'm glad that I told you about Roger. We were in law school together before the baby was born. And he reminds me a lot of Steven."

"Well, as long as you're happy. That's all that matters."

"You know, you're welcome to stay with us if you decide to come for a visit."

"No, that's okay. I can stay at a hotel not far from where you are. I wouldn't dream of imposing on you like that. Let me check with the airlines and call you right back."

"Okay, I'm hanging up now."

Courtney had sent a studio picture of her, Roger, and Lil' Roger to Dr. Palmer. He'd almost dropped the picture when he saw Roger's face. *He looks too much like Steven to be real. He's got those thick eyebrows and that dark curly hair just like my son. No wonder Courtney was attracted to him. Well, they say that everyone has a twin. He could surely pass for Steven's.*

Dr. Palmer couldn't stop looking at the picture, running his thumb over the outline of Roger's face. *How could he look so much like Steven?*

Finally, he placed the picture in his wallet and closed it up.

He hung up the telephone with Courtney and called American Airlines, making reservations to arrive in Houston in two weeks. He decided that enough time had passed without him seeing his grandson.

Dr. Palmer was also planning to check out the young man spending so much time around his grandchild. He didn't want just anybody hanging around his relatives.

I can't get over his resemblance to Steven. I definitely need to find out who this boy's relatives are.

Twenty minutes later, Dr. Palmer was calling Courtney back. "I'll be in town in two weeks. I plan to stay at a hotel near the Astrodome. I'm really anxious to hold my grandson."

"Oh, that's great. We're looking forward to seeing you too. He looks more like Steven everyday."

"He looks a lot like that young man in the pictures, too."
"That's what everyone says, Dr. Palmer."
"All right, I'll see you soon. Good night, Courtney."
"Good night, Dr. Palmer."

Chapter sixteen

"Daddy is sick." Majesta set up in bed, holding the telephone receiver to her ear. She was still half asleep as she looked over Alex, snoring.

"What's wrong with him?" she asked Kim, walking to the bathroom.

"Mama said he has a high temperature, and he's been throwing up all night. She's taking him to the emergency room."

"Are you going?"

"Yes, if you want to go, I'll pick you up."

"Okay, I'll get dressed and leave Ah'Shiyah here with Alex." She flushed the toilet, washed her hands, and went back in the bedroom to change.

Arriving at the hospital, they saw Jessica and their mother waiting in the lobby. Mr. Charles was being treated for a virus. The doctors wanted to keep him for forty-eight hours of observation.

When they went in to see him, Jessica burst into tears, ran to her daddy, and hugged him. If he had a cold, she would nurse him back to health because she's was daddy's little girl.

Sitting next to him, Jessica's eyes were still filled with tears. She rubbed the bald spot on his head and held his hand.

Mrs. Charles kissed her husband on the cheek and said, "I love you, honey. Don't try to talk."

Then she turned to the girls and said, "He needed to come to the hospital. I wasn't going to try to doctor on him this time."

Shortly after their arrival, Mr. Charles dozed off. Kim and Majesta were ready to leave. "We'll be back later, mama," Kim said.

Jessica and her mother stayed for a while longer talking about Mr. Charles and praying for him to get better.

"Mama, we have to take care of daddy. This is the second time this month he's been sick."

"Okay, Jessica."

Jessie kissed her dad, her mother, and then she went home. Mrs. Charles sat on the sofa next to her husband's bed, dozing off as well. This had been a trying time for her.

Later that day, Kim and Jessie gave Courtney a call. Courtney was bathing her baby when the telephone rang.

"Roger," she called. "Could you get that please?"

"I got it. Hello?"

"Hi, Roger, how's everybody?"

"Hi, Kim, we're all doing fine."

"I'm on the line, too," Jessica chimed in.

"Where is our sister?"

"She's giving Lil' Roger a bath."

"So we take it that she's doing better."

"Yes, she's much better now." He went on to tell them how Courtney had been attending therapy sessions once a week. And he explained that she was on another type of medication now to help with the OCD problem and how it helped her to deal with things getting messed up at times. "She takes off her shoes when she goes outside now. She still keeps the place spotless. She just doesn't wake up in the middle of the night to clean it."

Kim said, "Wow, that's good news."

"She's 100% better."

Kim responded saying, "She was placed on medication in high school for that problem. I'm glad to hear that she's finally getting over it."

Jessica interjected, "She had the cleanest room in the house. She thought everyone had germs and she put toilet paper on the seat, even at home."

"Yeah, we know how the medication can work. Just make sure she keeps on taking it. She was on it when she left home, but we believe she stopped while attending college. Make sure she doesn't drink any alcohol. That stuff makes her crazy."

"Okay, here's Courtney."

Roger passed the telephone to Courtney and took Lil' Roger into his arms. He left the room cradling the baby. Now that he was dressed, it was feeding time.

"I'm feeling better everyday. I've come a long way. I've learned so much about myself." She hadn't really talked to them since she came out of the hospital. Courtney remembered them calling, but she couldn't remember what they'd talked about.

Kim and Jessica told her about their dad. Then they reassured her that he was doing fine.

Courtney asked, "How's Majesta doing?"

Kim replied, "She's doing fine, and Ah'Shiyah is walking."

They talked on the telephone for almost an hour. Kim was paying for the call so she ended the conversation with, "It's been great catching up, but let's bring this to a close."

That night, Courtney and Roger talked about the visit Lil' Roger's grandfather was making the next week. "I don't know how he's going to feel about me taking his son's place."

"You're a wonderful father. I think that he'll be happy to see such a positive man in his grandchild's life. You're a Godsend to Lil' Roger and me. Thank you for taking me to the hospital."

Courtney was convinced that she was better off now than she was in high school. Her parents had taken her to some doctor who tried to help her with her problem. Only then, she didn't want help. This time she did. She found it hard to believe that she had a chemical glitch in the brain. After taking the medication for weeks, she noticed a change in her own behavior.

While she was hospitalized, Courtney learned that the bad thoughts she'd had of hurting her baby was also from her OCD. She thought that checking things, fear of contamination, and fretting over cleanliness were the only symptoms but some patients also suffer from bad thoughts as well.

She was thankful for Roger's help. Courtney didn't care about having to spend time at a mental institution or having it on her medical records. *I don't care what people think of me anymore. I'm forever grateful to Roger for saving my life. That shows how special he is.*

"Courtney, you should do your collages all the time and not just when you're upset. Fix up your picture room again. Make some more collages."

"I will. I still need to make one for your mother."

"Oh, yeah, she'll love it. That woman has got to have over a million pictures at her house," he joked.

They finished their conversation. Courtney could feel her medication beginning to work. It was making her drowsy as she made the way to her bed.

Roger stayed up watching basketball. He loved basketball, and so did his mother. They talked about the sport all the time. It didn't matter to them whether it was on the radio or television. They were always ready for a good game, and they especially loved those Houston Rockets.

Chapter seventeen

"Hi, Majesta, it's your sister, Courtney. I like your voice message on the answering machine. I was just calling to see how you were doing. I'm much better now, and I'd like to talk with you about some things."

Listening to the replay of Courtney's message, Alex wondered how he really felt about getting married to Majesta since they'd been living together the last month. There was a certain feeling in his heart as he listened to Courtney's voice on his answering machine. She sounded so intelligent, so sweet, and so sexy.

It had been years since he'd heard that magnificent voice, but he'd seen pictures of her. Majesta had only shown him a few pictures of Courtney. *She's as beautiful now as she was when we first met. She was just too trusting of me. She didn't think that I'd do anything wrong.*

Alex remembered how sweet Courtney always smelled and how she was always picture perfect with never a thing out of place. Majesta had told him why Courtney was like that. *She probably never would have kissed me if she hadn't been medicated back then. I hate it when Majesta calls her crazy.*

He knew that Majesta was jealous of her sister. Alex wondered if marrying her was a good idea since she had much animosity towards Courtney. It seemed even worse now that they were getting married.

Majesta hated the fact that she couldn't bring herself to tell Courtney about her engagement. Her sisters often told her, "You're wrong for being with Alex."

Majesta had stopped trying to find Nelson to pay child support. She felt like Alex was more a father to Ah'Shiyah than he'd ever be anyway. Alex saw him more than once, but he didn't tell Majesta because he didn't want to get involved. He loved Majesta and Ah'Shiyah. *Do I love Courtney, too? How would I feel about being in the same room with her?*

It was hard listening to Courtney's sweet voice on the answering machine. He hadn't realized how much he'd missed her over the years. He'd seen pictures of Courtney with the baby and Roger. She hadn't changed much. Courtney still had the large breasts that he'd loved. *I wish Majesta had a chest like that.*

They still hadn't decided on a date for the wedding. He told Majesta, "I want to finish college first so that I won't have to depend on my parents or yours to support us."

It was hard enough living in a small apartment that Majesta didn't like. She suggested that they move into a bigger place closer to her parents' house. Majesta didn't have any shame in asking her parents for money. She got money from them all the time.

Alex, on the other hand, was quick to let her folks know that he had a job and was paying rent. He didn't approve of Majesta spending all of her money shopping either. If they were going to make it as a couple, she'd have to make some changes.

Being a typical man, Alex couldn't help himself. He rewound the answering machine just to hear Courtney's voice again. *If she only knew how Majesta felt about her. She wouldn't be talking like that.*

Majesta had told him how she really felt about her relationship with Courtney. She whined about Courtney getting every man that she wanted before declaring, "She's not going to get you from me."

I wonder if Courtney ever got over me. She looks happy with Roger. Majesta said that he's good people and he'll do anything for Courtney.

Majesta filled him in on all of Courtney's blues. He knew all the details regarding her incident with Nelson, and the other men that had entered her life.

She's been through a lot in the past few years. I know that I was the reason for her first heartbreak, though. And I was wrong for what I did to her.

Alex felt strange thinking that one day Courtney would be his sister-in-law. They would be family after all.

He put on his tennis shoes, and then called his friends, Ryan and Melvin, so that they could meet him at the park to play some basketball. He needed to get his mind off of Courtney.

Ryan said, "Man, you're crazy marrying Majesta. You're not ready for marriage."

"Yeah," Melvin began, "You need to think twice about marrying your ex-girlfriend's sister."

Alex shrugged them off. Majesta and Ah'Shiyah were walking in as he hung up the telephone. It was noon and Majesta had already been to the store. She was just getting back from Sears.

Majesta shopped at the name brand retail stores and baby boutiques. The baby dressed better than she did.

Alex shook his head thinking to himself, *I can't imagine Courtney making a fuss over her son like that. He's probably a regular kid.*

"Hey, Courtney called while you were out."

"Really, what did she have to say?"

Alex relayed Courtney's message to Majesta. She didn't seem interested at all.

"It's probably still on the answering machine if you want to listen to it for yourself."

"Nah, that's okay. I'll call her later."

Alex kissed Majesta on the cheek. He picked up the baby and kissed her on the cheek, too. "I'll be back in about two hours. I'm going to play some b-ball."

"I want to go to the cafeteria for dinner."

"Fine," he replied, walking out the door.

Majesta placed Ah'Shiyah in her play pin with a cookie. Then she called Courtney to see what she wanted.

"Hi, sis, what's up?"

"Oh, I'm fine. I just hadn't heard from you lately. I talked to Kim and Jessie."

"I've been so busy. Ah'Shiyah keeps me going. Since she's been walking, it seems like she gets into everything. I had to rearrange my house for that little lady."

"Lil' Roger is crawling, and he's trying to pull up."

"Kim told me that Dr. Palmer is coming down to see him."

"Yes, he's also planning to relocate here. He said he wants the baby to know his Grandpa."

Something in Majesta made her want to spill the beans about her engagement to Alex. She was tired of keeping her love life a secret from Courtney.

"I've got something to share with you. Kim and Jessie both told me that I shouldn't tell you, but I just want to be honest."

"What is it? You can tell me anything."

And Majesta let it all out in one long breath. "Alex and I have been dating for awhile now, and we're engaged to be married."

Courtney couldn't speak. Feeling a lump in her throat, she blinked her eyes. *Did I just hear her correctly? Did Majesta say that she was dating and getting married to my first love, Alex? How could she be so cruel? Out of all the men in Miami, she hooks up with Alex.*

"Majesta, how could you do that to me? You know how I felt about Alex. It took me a long time to get over him breaking up with me. He really hurt me."

"Listen, Courtney, I love Alex, and he loves me. I thought you were in love with Roger. You two are planning to marry."

"I know. I'm just saying that Alex was…"

"He came after me," Majesta lied. "I was lonely. I'm sorry for hurting you. We're an item. If you can't handle it, then that's too bad."

Courtney couldn't believe how selfish her baby sister had become. She was finally showing how jealous she'd always been of Courtney.

Majesta was almost happy that Courtney took the news hard. *It serves her right. She's just upset because she can't have him.*

Courtney said, "I'm not happy about your engagement. I probably won't be attending the wedding or visiting you all."

"If that's what you want, so be it."

Fighting the anger in her voice, Courtney replied, "Think about what you're doing. Good-bye."

Roger overheard the end of the conversation between the two of them. He walked in the living room asking, "What was that fuss all about?"

Courtney acted like nothing was wrong, but Roger could see that she was visibly disturbed about something. Majesta had said something to hurt her. He'd heard the name Alex mentioned before. *He was Courtney's first love. Majesta told me that Courtney never got over him.*

Walking by Roger, Courtney went to her bedroom. She was so angry with her sister that she couldn't stand it. She couldn't control her feelings.

She didn't have it in her to tell Roger what was really going on. This had to be the worst news she had heard since Steven's death. It was hard imagining Alex as her brother-in-law.

This has got to be a joke. Majesta is not crazy enough to do such a thing. She's doing this to get back at me. She's bitter about all the things that happened in her love life.

Courtney couldn't believe that Alex was in love with Majesta. Her sister had to be lying. Courtney closed the bedroom door, picked up the telephone, and called Jessica. *I'm not being fair to Roger, but I have to know the truth.*

Jessica wasn't home so she dialed Kim's number. Carlton answered the telephone.

"Hi, Carlton, is Kim home? I need to talk to her, it's very important."

"She's not home. She's working at the shop."

Courtney was desperate. "Carlton, do you know who Majesta's dating now?"

Carlton was quiet for several seconds. She asked him again. This time he replied, "His name is Alex."

Feeling weak, Courtney could hardly hold the receiver. It was true. Majesta was really engaged to Alex. Her sister had betrayed her. Majesta didn't love her anymore. *I can't believe that Kim and Jessica didn't tell me about this nightmare.*

At that moment, Roger opened the door asking, "What's wrong with you?"

"I'm all right. Just give me a minute, please," she said to Roger, raising a hand. Then she spoke into the telephone receiver saying, "Thanks, Carlton. I have to go now, good-bye."

Roger closed the door and returned to the living room with Lil' Roger.

Courtney swallowed one of her pills without water, pulled the covers back, and got in bed with her clothes still on. She laid her head against the pillow thinking about Alex.

Remembering their past, she recalled how she used to sneak him over to her house while her mother was taking her father to physical therapy. It was during the summertime when school was out. Her parents left the house around nine o'clock every other morning.

She wasn't allowed to have her boyfriend over when her parents weren't home, but she and her sisters did. Alex came over to their house every morning that her parents were out.

He would ride his bike over to see her. She would have her room clean and tidy. They would pretend that her room was their own place. Alex was her first boyfriend, and the first guy that she'd ever French kissed.

One day, they decided to get naked. He started off by showing his chest to her. Then she pulled down her sundress, and showed him hers. He almost lost his mind staring at her full breasts.

He kicked off his shoes and socks. Then he removed his pants standing in the middle of the room, showing his white Fruit of the Loom underwear.

Sliding her sundress down over her hips, Courtney tossed it on the bed along with her panties. Standing buck naked in front of him, she could see his lower body react.

Alex reached out his hand, pulling Courtney close to him. They kissed a little, enjoying only the taste of each other's mouths.

Although they remained virgins, they spent the remainder of the summer lusting over each other. It became routine for them to get undressed, get in bed, and kiss without having intercourse.

Courtney had been afraid to take things any further. She was satisfied with just grinding against one another.

About a year later, Alex was ready for more. "I love you, Courtney. Can we take it to the next level?" he begged.

"I can't."

"I want us to connect. You know, become one."

"Then we should get married."

"I think we need to have sex first," he pressed. "You know, try it out."

Courtney was nervous. Her sister, Kim, had told her how bad it would hurt the first time. So initially she refused to have sex with him by saying, "I'm not ready."

Alex starting kissing her in places he hadn't kissed before. Soon Courtney was relaxed enough to let him have his way with her. The tenseness she felt at first quickly dissolved as they made love on top of the bed.

When they finished, Courtney pulled the sheets off her bed and washed them. She ran a tub of water and scrubbed herself until she felt clean again.

A warm feeling came over Courtney as she remembered her first love. She imagined Alex and her making love like they had done so many times in the past. Courtney realized that she'd never gotten over him.

She'd kept her feelings locked up inside of herself. Dawson was someone who helped her forget. He was always thinking of things to do and different places to go. She found herself not thinking of Alex so much.

Then Steven came along. She really loved him. He didn't have to give her anything but himself. He had been all she needed. He had good looks, great hygiene, and when they made love, what a feeling! It was better than her first time. He was the one man who really could have replaced Alex.

The only two men Courtney ever wanted belonged to someone else. Majesta had Alex and Steven was with God. Roger, on the other hand, was good, but Courtney realized that she didn't love him like she had loved Alex and Steven.

She wasn't planning to attend Majesta and Alex's wedding, that was for sure. *I really don't want to have anything to do with Majesta.*

Roger entered the room with Lil' Roger in his arms. The baby had fallen asleep while watching television.

He placed Lil' Roger in his crib. Then he got into the bed with Courtney. She pretended to be asleep as he snuggled up next to her, hoping to become intimate. He placed tender kisses on the back of her neck.

"I'm tired, Roger. I'm not in the mood," she mumbled, inching closer to the edge of the bed.

"What's the matter?"

Courtney turned and faced him. "I'm just tired. The medication makes me sleepy. Let me get a little shut eye, and then maybe later we can make love."

"Okay, sweetheart, I can wait."

He rolled over and went to sleep like an obedient child. He was too nice to her and had always shown love towards her son. Roger was about four years older than she was, and smarter, too. He had answers to everything and usually made good decisions. Courtney could see the God in him. He had really changed her life.

Roger had told her, "It's wrong of us to live together without being married." He wanted to marry her as soon as possible. Roger went to church with or without her every Sunday. God was first in his life. He read the Bible along with his law books daily. He was indeed a man of God.

I just wish that I was more like him. I pray that God will bless me to have the utmost faith in Him. I pray that God will plant His seed in my heart while I'm young. I want that same joy that Roger has and shows on many occasions. I pray that God will bless Roger to find his father.

Courtney knew that Roger wondered about his father, whether he was dead or alive. Sometimes she felt sorry for him because he had often told her, "I wish that my father had loved my mother like I love you."

Running her fingers through his curly hair, Courtney could say that he was the sweetest person she'd ever known. She felt that Roger would find heaven. She hoped that she could get herself together so that she could find heaven as well. She said another before drifting off to sleep.

"Dear Heavenly Father, I pray that you will give me the mind of your son, Jesus Christ. Fix my heart to love You first, Lord. Help me to keep my mind stayed on Jesus. And help me to reach my goal, which is to have a wonderful God-fearing life. Thank you for hearing my prayer and I look forward to eternal peace with You in Your house. Amen."

When Courtney woke up the next morning, Roger was already preparing breakfast. He often did that on the weekend. She could smell the fresh brewing coffee. When Courtney got up, she saw Lil' Roger trudging along in his walker. He could get around well in it, too.

Roger made bacon, eggs, biscuits, and grits for breakfast. And boy was she hungry.

"Good morning," he said, giving her a kiss on the cheek.

"Good morning, Roger." She went back in the room to put on her housecoat. Then she made up the bed, brushed her teeth, and got washed up.

By the time she made it back in the kitchen, breakfast was on the table. Roger sat down and they held hands while he said the grace. He could pray well, and he normally prayed in church during altar call.

Roger concluded his prayer and they began to eat. He was certainly a good cook, just like his mother.

Courtney remembered how Steven used to fix her breakfast. He couldn't cook like Roger, but he loved to do little things like that. That was one thing they had in common; they both liked to serve their lady. They loved to please Courtney.

"Kim called you this morning."

"She did? I didn't hear the phone ring."

"I turned off the ringer in your room so that you could get some rest."

"You are always thinking about me. I really don't deserve you, Roger."

He smiled, winking his eye at her. Lil' Roger had already eaten his breakfast. He was sitting in his walker sucking his juice bottle.

Courtney rushed down her food so that she could call Kim and talk to her about Majesta. She didn't need Alex. He was wrong for being with her sister. *That goes to show how much he cares about our relationship as sisters. And Majesta is acting like we're not even related.*

Courtney washed up the dishes and wiped down everything in the kitchen. Then she took Lil' Roger out of his walker and put him in his crib. He was already sleeping soundly.

"I'm headed to church. Are you sure you don't feel up to going with me today?"

"No, I can't make it today."

"Okay, I'm going to run by my mother's house after service. I also need to stop at the grocery store to pick up a few things on my way home."

Courtney was glad that he was leaving. She had a lot of talking to do with Kim and Jessica.

Maybe it was the pills or her prayer, but she wasn't as bothered about Majesta's pending engagement to Alex this morning. She had a lot to be thankful for in her own life without worrying about them.

After cleaning up for a bit, she sat down on the sofa, and did a three-way telephone call to Kim and Jessie. She was a little surprised to find both of them home on a Sunday.

Jessica told them that she had gotten home late last night from her date with Paul. She was still messing around with William, too. He'd spent the night several times since their hot love making session on the kitchen floor.

Paul was a dependable guy, but Jessie had decided to break-up with him. It just wasn't fair to be sleeping with this man while she was still undecided about the future of her marriage.

Courtney chatted with them about their lives before bringing up the subject of Majesta and Alex. "I know about Majesta's latest fling."

Kim said, "Carlton told me about your phone call. It's not a fling. They're planning their wedding and everything."

Jessie replied, "I'm not going to be in the wedding. It just doesn't feel right."

"How about you, Kim? How do you feel about this situation?"

Kim hesitated several seconds, and then replied, "Courtney, I really don't think it's in good taste. I suggested to Majesta that they elope. She got mad at me when I said that so it's not happening. Mom and dad don't like it either. They already live in an apartment close to mama and daddy."

Jessica said, "Ah'Shiyah calls him daddy. They act like they're already married."

Courtney couldn't take in all of this information. It was too much for her to bear. Kim and Jessica asked, "How are you taking the news?"

She was honest with her sisters. She told them, "It hurts. But what can I do? I'm planning to get married, too. I'll probably be married by the time I come back to Miami so I'll just have to deal with it."

Courtney talked on the telephone for almost an hour, crying with her sisters. She finally said good-bye to them. Then she hung up and cried herself to sleep.

Roger came home and found her sleeping on the sofa with Lil' Roger lying in his crib. He put the grocery bags down, changed the baby, and put him in his walker. He was putting the groceries away when Courtney woke up and started helping him.

"How's your mom?"

"She's doing well. She asked me when the baby's grandfather was coming down."

"He should be down next Friday night at seven. Roger, I want to get married. Let's elope before he comes. I'm really ready to marry you. Let's not live in sin anymore. Marry me, Roger, I love you."

Roger stopped what he was doing to hug and kiss Courtney. He'd been waiting for this since Lil' Roger's birth. He was beginning to think that Courtney didn't want to marry him. He ran to the room to retrieve the ring he'd bought for her.

All Courtney could do was cry. This was one special man. Nobody but God had given her Roger. He was indeed a Godsend.

Chapter eighteen

Dr. Palmer had everything packed. He made some calls to several realtors searching for a location for his new office. He would do more than visit his grandson. On this trip, he had to find an apartment as well as a storage place for his belongings. Later, he would look for a suitable home. First, he wanted to get to Houston.

He was hoping that Texas would agree with him. But then again, it really didn't matter because he was doing this just to be near his grandson. Steven Roger was all he had.

Dr. Palmer called Courtney again to make sure that she would be at the airport to meet him. He'd already made hotel reservations at the Astro Hotel next to the Astrodome Complex. This would put him in the heart of the city.

Mrs. Williams was preparing dinner for them on Saturday; Dr. Palmer was looking forward to that. Courtney had told him that she was widowed like him. *I think maybe Courtney is trying to be a match maker. I wouldn't mind a little female company in a new city.*

Dr. Palmer was a handsome man for his age. Considering that he was an OB/GYN, he was used to seeing a lot of women and being set-up. Some of his own patients tried to hit on him. But he was looking forward to meeting a strong Texas woman. Courtney told him that Mrs. Williams was born and raised in North Carolina. *At least we'll have something in common. I'll work a half day tomorrow and come home before catching my afternoon flight.*

He checked his messages and then retired for the evening. Although he wasn't sure if he'd be able to get any sleep. Dr. Palmer closed his eyes and waited to see what would happen.

Courtney bought a lacy beige dress, met Reverend Reid at the church with Roger's family, and recited her marriage vows while holding Lil' Roger in her arms. It was just like a movie scene that she'd seen before. When they both said, "I do," she handed the baby to Roger. "Now we're a family," she whispered.

All of Roger's siblings attended the wedding including his sister, Samantha. She was the first to hug the bride and say, "Welcome to the family, Courtney. I hope that you and my brother will be very happy."

Roger walked around with his head held high. He looked so proud to be a husband and father. As soon as the ceremony ended, they headed to Mrs. Williams' house to feast on one of her great meals and cut their wedding cake.

Later that evening, Courtney called Dr. Palmer to share the good news. "Roger and I got married today. We didn't want to wait any longer."

"That's wonderful. I'm pleased to know that you're happy. It's not good for anyone to be alone. Roger seems to be a decent man. I enjoyed our conversation the other day."

"Thank you for being so understanding about this. Roger and Lil' Roger will be with me when I pick you up at the airport." Majesta crossed her mind for a second, but she quickly dismissed any thoughts of her sister and Alex. She had to concentrate on the meeting of a grandson and grandfather. That was the most important thing to her.

Roger was nervous and excited about meeting Dr. Palmer. "Sure, he sounded nice over the phone, but how do you think he'll react to seeing me in person?"

"I think everything is going to be fine. He'll be happy to see that you're a wonderful father to his grandchild."

At Hobby Airport, Courtney waited with Roger and Lil' Roger for Dr. Palmer's airplane to arrive. She'd almost forgotten how he looked until she saw a middle aged dark skinned, curly haired man wearing blue jeans and a red shirt walking towards her. He favored Steven from a distance.

Roger looked at Dr. Palmer like he'd seen a ghost. This man looked like family. For some reason, Roger felt relaxed as Dr. Palmer drew closer to them.

After seeing Roger's face, Dr. Palmer made a mental note to check his past. He was so shaken by seeing Roger that he almost didn't notice his handsome grandson dressed up in a navy outfit, smelling clean and fresh.

The emotions that he felt were too great to be contained. Dr. Palmer released a stream of tears, reaching for his grandson. He held the baby close to his heart and closed his eyes. Courtney started crying at the site of them together. This moment was exactly like she'd dreamed it would be. She turned to look at Roger and noticed a tear in the corner of his eye.

Dr. Palmer kissed his grandson on the cheek, and held him like a teddy bear. He couldn't stop staring at this amazing little boy that shared his blood. Roger took his bag, walking behind him and Courtney towards the parked car. They drove him to the hotel, stayed for a short while, and then left.

Courtney and Roger talked about Dr. Palmer all night long. Roger said, "At first I was really nervous about meeting him, but the second I saw him, I felt totally relaxed. It was strange."

"Well, I'm glad that you two got along as well as you did. I knew you didn't have anything to worry about."

"I know I'm tired. It was really a draining day for me since I wasn't sure what to expect from our meeting."

"Didn't you say that you were born in North Carolina?"

"That's what my mother told me."

A thought came to Courtney, but she didn't tell Roger what it was. He would have to wait.

The next morning, Courtney called Dr. Palmer to see how he slept his first night in Houston. "Did you sleep okay, Dr. Palmer?"

"Yes, I did. I was so tired from the flight and the excitement from seeing my grandson left me exhausted. I'm getting old. I can't handle all of that excitement," he said, laughing at himself.

Courtney laughed with him. Then she said, "Don't forget that we're eating dinner at my mother-in-law's house."

"Just call me before you leave your house, and I'll meet you in the hotel lobby. How's my grandson?"

"Oh, he's a little fussy today, but he'll be all right."

"I'll see you when you get here. I can't wait to hold the baby again."

Courtney hung up the telephone and called Mrs. Williams to see if she needed them to bring anything, but she wasn't home. Roger said, "My mama is probably at the store shopping."

"Yeah, you're right. I'll just leave a message on her answering machine."

She picked out a cute outfit for Lil' Roger and got him changed. "What are you wearing, Roger?"

"I'm wearing my gray pants with a black and gray shirt."

Courtney picked out a denim pants suit with a black suede collar. She put on suede shoes to match. Glancing at herself in the full length mirror, she bent down to pick up the ringing telephone.

"Hi, Courtney, I just missed your call. I was bringing the groceries in."

"That's okay. I was just calling to see what time you wanted us to be there for dinner and to see if you needed us to bring anything."

"I don't need you to bring anything but an appetite. Dinner will be served at five o'clock."

When they made it to the hotel, Dr. Palmer was waiting for them in the lobby. Roger shook his hand as Courtney smiled at them. He could feel the older gentlemen staring at him when he turned to open the hotel lobby door for Courtney on their way out.

Dr. Palmer climbed into the back seat of Roger's sedan and sat next to the baby. He played with him the whole way to Mrs. Williams' house. This was turning out to be a very pleasant trip.

They arrived at Mrs. Williams' house at 4:15. Roger honked the horn as they pulled up into the driveway. He and Courtney got out of the car, walked to the front door, and knocked.

Dr. Palmer got the baby out of his car seat as Courtney and Roger entered the house. Courtney held the door open, waiting patiently for them.

Mrs. Williams walked out of the kitchen wearing mittens and holding a hot apple pie in her hands. She was about to place it on the table as Courtney said, "Mrs. Williams, I'd like to introduce you to…"

She dropped the pie before Courtney could finish the sentence. She was standing in the middle of the floor between the living room and dining area. The apple pie was turned upside down on the wooden floor.

"Oh, my Lord, it can't be true."

Dr. Palmer looked at her with his mouth opened. *This can't be Teresa Johnson. I haven't seen her in years, but she looks just as pretty as she did in high school.* "Teresa, is that you?"

Roger and Courtney were looking at them, clearly not understanding what was going on. Mrs. Williams ran to her room and slammed the door. This seemed like a dream. The dream that she'd prayed would happen some day. Only now she was so embarrassed that she didn't know what to do. *Oh, sweet Jesus. Help me please. I've got to get back out there to my guests.*

While she was getting herself together, Dr. Palmer took a seat on the sofa as Roger gave him the third degree. "What's going on? Do you know my mother?"

"Yes, we dated for a while in high school."

Roger looked at Dr. Palmer closely. This time it was like looking into a mirror. It was clear to him now what was going on. He felt anger and happiness at the same time. "Are you my father?"

Dr. Palmer opened his mouth to speak, but Mrs. Williams walked back into the living room with a handkerchief, drying her teary eyes. Without speaking, she looked at Roger and then turned to Dr. Palmer.

He'd never thought twice when Teresa told him that she was pregnant. "It's not mine," he'd angrily declared. He had heard that story too many times to believe it. She dropped out of school and he started dating Dorita Clark. He hadn't given Teresa another thought until today.

Standing up, Dr. Palmer handed Lil' Roger to Courtney. This was too much for him to handle. Roger looked more like him than his deceased son. There wasn't any denying that. Roger looked at Dr. Palmer with tears in his eyes, causing Courtney and Mrs. Williams to weep also. He walked over to Dr. Palmer and hugged him.

Dr. Palmer looked at Mrs. Williams as he returned Roger's hug. She smiled at him for a second then looked away.

Being a law student, Roger made a suggestion. "I think that we should have a blood test done just to be sure. I mean, I'd like to have official proof that you're my father."

Dr. Palmer hesitated a moment before replying, "Well, I guess we could do that. It wouldn't hurt to make it official."

Mrs. Williams was offended. Folding her arms across her chest, she said, "You'll just be wasting your time and money. Everybody here can see that. You don't need a blood test to see who your daddy is."

"Mom, please, I'm not questioning you. I just need it to be official."

"It's your money, be my guest."

One thing was real; no one cared about eating anything that evening. They all sat in the living room crying and talking, talking and crying until the evening was over.

No one ever blamed Dr. Palmer for his actions. Somehow, Roger understood. He'd had a girlfriend to tell him the same thing years ago; fortunately it turned out that she was lying.

Being a Christian, he knew that the right thing to do was to forgive and move on with his life. Mrs. Williams felt the same way.

Courtney was the only one in shock. She'd managed to find her baby's uncle and marry him. This was unreal. She'd reunited father and son as well as two high school sweethearts. *I could write a book about this. This should be on a talk show. Stuff like this could make a person crazy.* Courtney sat on the sofa, crying as she held her baby close. Everyone was drained from this experience.

Before they retired that evening, Roger said a prayer in the living room. "Thank you, God, for this wonderful day. I pray that we can all get along, that my father and I will grow to love one another, and that You will bless us all in the days to come."

Later on that night, Courtney and Roger left the baby at Mrs. Williams' house and drove Dr. Palmer back to his hotel room.

They rode in silence the entire way there. Once Dr. Palmer entered the hotel lobby, Courtney and Roger returned to Mrs. William's house and slept in Roger's old room.

They talked until after two o'clock in the morning. Roger reminded Courtney, "You need to take your medicine. Something like this could really give you a setback."

Courtney complied with his wishes. She kept her pills with her at all times.

"Roger, Steven was your brother. Lil' Roger is your nephew. It's unreal."

"We were meant to be. Thanks to you, I found my dad."

He kissed her, and they lay in each other's arms until they fell asleep. It had been an unbelievable day.

Dr. Palmer felt that Roger was his son. He didn't need a blood test; he now trusted Teresa's word. Yet, he knew it was best to make it official so that they could all move on with their lives.

She never messed around on me. She was in love with me. Teresa was just too proud to ask me for anything. Not once did she call me or come by my house. When she told me that she was pregnant, I told her that it wasn't mine. She just looked at me in disbelief and walked away. And she never came back to school after that day.

He just hadn't loved her enough to care. He was young, and he simply didn't have time for love. All he cared about was having sex and having money. But Dr. Palmer had changed his life since that time.

When he met his wife in college, he was finished fooling around, clubbing, and smoking weed. He was ready for marriage and starting a family. *Maybe this is a second chance for me to do the right thing. Could Teresa ever love me again?*

Seeing her looking so good, and knowing that she'd given birth to his son made him want her. *She's done a wonderful job raising Roger. He's such a fine young man. And he's been raising his nephew. This seems like a dream. Here I am trying to be with my grandson when I find out that I have a son that I never knew about. That explains why the baby looks so much like Roger.*

Mrs. Williams was in her room thinking about the turn in the day's events. Her first love had come back to her, and she didn't even have to look for him. Seeing Kool-Aid really brought back those first time feelings, their first meeting, their first kiss, their first sex, and the first pregnancy.

She had to find a job after the baby was born. Her parents refused to baby-sit or do anything to help Teresa out. They provided food and shelter and that was about it. They never took her earnings, but they never let her forget that she'd had a baby out of wedlock.

Both of her parents died later on that year, and she moved to Georgia, then Texas. There, she soon met her now deceased husband who raised Roger as his own.

Now, all these years later, her first love was here in town. What a wonderful blessing.

Chapter nineteen

"Happy birthday to you! Happy birthday to you!" The entire crowd was singing.

It was Lil' Roger's first birthday. Mrs. Williams made him a vanilla cake with blue and green frosting then placed a red race car in the center.

All of Roger's sisters and brothers, along with their children, were there. Dr. Palmer had started his practice in Sugarland, Texas, and had a home in Missouri City which was only fifteen minutes away.

Dr. Palmer and Mrs. Williams had become good friends. They even attended the same church. Courtney was also attending church with them every Sunday now even though she hadn't been to Florida to see her family. It had been almost a year since she'd last seen her parents.

She was planning to take Roger and Lil' Roger to Miami in three months. By that time, Majesta and Alex would be married.

Kim and Jessica had filled her in on the wedding arrangements. They had both given in and decided to be a part of the ceremony. Courtney still hadn't talked to Majesta since she'd learned about the engagement. She really didn't have much to say to her baby sister. *I wish them the best. Maybe they can find happiness like I have.*

Roger prayed silently as his family sang *Happy Birthday* to *his son. Thank you, God, for my family. I pray that Lil' Roger will have many more happy birthdays. And thank you, God, for bringing my father to me. I'm eternally grateful for this blessing.*

Everyone passed Lil' Roger around, holding and kissing

him as he moved from one set of hands to the next. He was the youngest grandchild and already spoiled.

Courtney was very proud of her family. She'd been cutting out pictures for her next family collage. And she'd been sitting up every night cutting out pictures she'd taken the last couple of months. Her family in Miami had recently sent pictures, too.

Even Majesta had the nerve to send her a picture of her new family with Alex and Ah'Shiyah. It still hurt Courtney to see them together. Somehow, she'd have to get past it, though.

This would be a big collage. She bought a poster-size wooden frame. Courtney was hoping that it would be completed by next month.

In her therapy, she had told Dr. Winters about all the things that she'd been through with her family. The doctor told her, "It'll be good therapy for you to do this special collage. You should even include Majesta and Alex in it."

Dr. Winters was right, she needed to accept reality. Alex would be family. He would be her brother-in-law. *Life can't get any stranger than that.*

Everyone went home after the party was over. She and Roger opened up Lil' Roger's gifts for him. She waited until the party was over to open gifts that her family had sent.

Kim and her family sent toys and clothes. Her parents sent him five pairs of shoes. Jessica sent him six outfits. Majesta sent him a card with fifty dollars in it.

Roger's family gave him toys, clothes, and money, too. Dr. Palmer got him a powered three-wheel cycle which Courtney thought was too much for a baby.

Mrs. Williams offered them money, but they refused to take it. "Please keep your money. You've done enough for us already. We have a babysitter whenever we need it." Courtney was a part of a blessed family.

She decided to call her family before it got too late to thank them for their presents. She called her parents first, Jessica second, and Kim last.

Roger said, "You need to call Majesta, too. I understand you're uncomfortable with her, but it's best to let it go. If you truly love me, you'll move past this."

Courtney shook her head indicating that wouldn't be an easy task. She buried her face in her hands, sitting at the foot of the bed.

"You know, you should go to the wedding and face the facts."

"I can't. I'll wait until it's over to go down there," she insisted.

She just didn't want to see her sister marry her first love. Courtney didn't mind if someone else married Alex. It was just hard to see a member of her family with him.

Roger left the room to let Courtney call her baby sister. It troubled him that Courtney was bothered by this ordeal. He had put her first, ahead of his own mother, but it didn't seem as though she'd done the same. Deep down in his heart, Roger knew that Courtney still had feelings for Alex. *I hope that one day she'll finally get that guy out of her system.*

She had everything: a husband who loved her, a beautiful son. And now that she was getting treatment for her OCD, she didn't fuss that much about the apartment being out of order.

Courtney called Majesta and to her surprise, Alex answered the telephone. "May I speak to Majesta?"

"Sure, hold on a second." He didn't even recognize Courtney's voice. It just sounded like an angry woman on the line.

"Hi, Majesta, I'm calling to thank you for the gift you sent Lil' Roger."

"You're welcome. Are you coming to my wedding?"

"No, I can't make it. I'll have to catch you later."

"Well, ah, congratulations on your marriage to Roger."

Majesta wanted to know more about what was happening in her sister's life. Courtney didn't feel like sharing the details with someone that she didn't really want to talk with. So she said, "I have to go, Majesta. Good-bye."

Majesta and Courtney couldn't seem to get their sisterly relationship back on track. It seemed like yesterday that they weren't speaking because of the rape. Now here was another man coming between then. *I wonder where Nelson is. He's never even seen Ah'Shiyah. If he did, he would know that she's his child. The older she gets the more she looks like him.*

By the time she got off the telephone, Roger and Lil' Roger were in bed. At two o'clock in the morning, Courtney woke up with an urge to work on her collage. She cut out twenty photographs and put them in the box where she kept her cut-out pictures.

Courtney walked to the closet and started unpacking her pictures. She was ready for her picture room again. Then she opened the taped boxes with her photo books. There were so many, and she still had pictures to put in photo albums.

When Roger woke up, he found Courtney in the picture room he'd been waiting to see. He had heard about all of her pictures. But seeing was believing, it was indeed a beautiful room.

Courtney lay on the floor asleep. Roger looked around the room at all the pictures. Some were framed, some were in collages, and some were in huge photo albums. She just had pictures everywhere.

This was truly a picture room with wall to wall pictures. *She must have started this collection when she was a child.*

"I used to always carry a camera with me."

Roger was startled at the sound of Courtney's voice. He turned to face her standing behind him.

"I got my first camera while I was in middle school as a birthday present. I still have it in a box with about eight other cameras."

Roger wanted to show this room to his parents. He decided to invite them over to dinner that evening. The paternity tests were scheduled to be completed this afternoon. He could pick up the results on his way home and celebrate the good news tonight with his wife and parents.

Chapter twenty

Carrying the blood test results in his hand, Roger was overjoyed to be home. He'd felt a little nervous earlier in the day when he went by the clinic to pick-up the results. Now his face was flushed with happiness, and his joy could be seen for miles. This was going to be the one of the greatest days of his life. He'd finally know how it felt to have a birth father.

Courtney and his mom had the table set using gold plated silverware with a fresh floral centerpiece and were ready for their dinner celebration. Dr. Palmer was sitting in front of the television set watching the news, holding the remote control in his hand.

Inhaling the aroma of pot roast, with vegetables, cornbread, and sweet potato pie, Roger spoke to everyone, and then looked directly at Mrs. Williams. "Mom, I've got the paternity test results right here," he declared, waving the envelope in the air.

"Oh, don't be silly. You don't need that to know who your father is. Why don't you give it to me and just let me hold on to it?" Mrs. Williams reached for the envelope. Roger turned his back to her, stepping towards the living room.

"No, no, this is what I've waited for my whole life. I need to know for myself that Dr. Palmer is my father and these tests will prove that beyond a reasonable doubt."

"Well, let's eat first. That can wait until later. Dinner is getting cold."

"That's all right, mama. After I read these results, we can heat the food up and really get down tonight."

Courtney said, "Let's all have a seat in the living room."

"Yeah, yeah, let's do that. Come on mom and dad."

Courtney took a seat beside Roger on the love seat, holding the baby on her lap. Mrs. Williams and Dr. Palmer were seated on the sofa; both had looks of anticipation stapled on their faces. Dr. Palmer was on the edge of his seat waiting for the joyous confirmation while Mrs. Williams was smiling and fiddling with her hands.

Roger tore into the envelope with the unparalleled excitement of a two-year-old boy on Christmas Day. His eyes glanced over the results in a matter of seconds.

"Th—th—this says that you're not my father. How can that be? We look just alike. What's going on here? Did they make a mistake?"

All eyes turned to Mrs. Williams. She covered her face with her hands and released a wailing sound loud enough to break glass. The tears flowed down her face like a gushing waterfall.

Courtney put the baby down and rushed to her mother-in-law's side. "Mrs. Williams, please try to calm down. We just want to know what's going on."

Dr. Palmer was stunned. He didn't know what to think of this. *Could that test be wrong? Teresa didn't seem like the type to fool around in high school. She was my girl.*

Roger handed his mother a paper towel to wipe the tears from her face. "Mom, please, tell us the truth. Who's my real father?"

She blew her nose and sniffled a few times before answering him. "If—if I tell the truth, Samuel will hate me forever. I can't—I can't do that."

"Teresa, come on. I could never hate you. So you made a mistake. We were young. We both made mistakes."

Turning to look directly into Roger's face, Teresa dried her tears, and spoke. "Stanley Palmer is your father."

Roger shouted, "Who is that?"

Courtney intervened, "Baby, don't shout at your mother. Calm down and let her speak, please."

Dr. Palmer stated, "He's my brother. How could you? How could you sleep with my own brother?"

"I was angry with you, Samuel. I told you that I was pregnant to test your love for me and you failed. You dismissed me like I was a piece of garbage. I slept with Stanley a few days later out of spite. Only I ended up getting pregnant for real that time. That's why I dropped out of school and never tried to contact either of you again. I was too embarrassed to admit what I'd done."

"Teresa, I don't know what to say. I've got to get out of here. I've got to get out of here right now." Dr. Palmer turned away from the scene, walked out the front door, and headed down the street.

Courtney screamed, "Roger, go get him! Don't let him leave like this. He's not your father, but he's still related to you. He doesn't need to be wandering around the streets in his condition."

"Okay, I'll go after him. You stay here with mama."

Mrs. Williams rested her head on Courtney's shoulder and said, "God forgive me. I'm glad that everything's finally out in the open."

Later that month, Majesta and Alex Reyes tied the knot in Miami. It was a big beautiful wedding in forest green and black. Majesta invited all of her friends and relatives. Alex's folks came from Belize, and Majesta was a picture perfect bride.

They had at least 200 people at the New Bethel Church, and the reception was held by the beach. With a live band playing in the background, she and Alex danced the night away on the white sand.

Courtney brought her family to Miami a week later. She saw Majesta and Alex at a reception at her parents' house that was held in honor of her and Roger.

At the sight of them together, Courtney almost broke out into hives. She couldn't hide the way that she felt. Her ears and chest turned red. She could feel Alex staring at her as he approached them.

Alex said, "Congratulations on your wedding." He shook Roger's hand. Then he kissed Courtney on the cheek. It was an uncomfortable feeling for her. She wanted this nightmare to end.

Majesta didn't have much to say to Courtney. She only saw the couple about three times the entire nine days that they were in Miami, and that was enough for her. Courtney loved her family, but she was ready to get back to Texas.

The last day they were in town, they met everyone at her parent's house to say their good-byes. Courtney cried the whole hour it took them to part.

Jessica said, "I'm coming to visit you for Christmas."

Kim chimed in, "Me, too. We can bring the kids and have a good time."

"That would be great. Roger and I would love to have you all."

Majesta and Alex didn't say anything about visiting them, and Courtney was happy that they didn't. She didn't have it in her heart to offer them an invitation. *Roger wouldn't mind, he's so open-minded about everything. But I just can't do it.*

Chapter twenty-one

While Courtney and Roger were gone, Mrs. Williams and Dr. Palmer had reconciled. They'd even gone out on a couple of dates to the movies, the park, and to his place. Teresa felt like a young woman again. It had been so long since a man had held her in his arms; it was a wonderful feeling.

She never imagined that she would actually be with Kool-Aid Palmer again. Only he wasn't Kool-Aid to her anymore, he was a decent man named Dr. Samuel Palmer. And she was falling in love with him all over again. *Will he ever be able to forgive me for deceiving him?*

Dr. Palmer hadn't dated anyone since his wife's death. Dating was something that he'd been determined to avoid especially with the women that he met on his job. He just wasn't ready for this modern day dating thing.

Now things were different with Teresa. He finally realized that he couldn't blame her for her actions anymore than he could blame himself for his. *We were both so young. We both made so many mistakes. If I can change my life, so can she.*

It was amazing how things had turned out. Roger was Dr. Palmer's nephew, and Lil' Roger was Roger's second cousin. Dr. Palmer looked back over his life thinking to himself, *Life is something else.*

They were sitting in the living room at his house watching television on the sofa. He reached out to Teresa and asked, "May I hold your hand?"

Teresa extended a hand to him with a smile. Taking her hand into his, he said, "I'm sorry for the hurt and embarrassment that I caused you in high school. I don't blame you for what happened, and I don't care about the past anymore. All I care about is having a future with you. Is that too much to ask?"

Mrs. Williams looked into his pleading eyes and said, "No, it's not. Thank you for forgiving me. I hope that we can have a bright future together."

Dr. Palmer trembled and Teresa felt it in his hand. She asked, "What's wrong?"

He turned away from her staring eyes. It would take a second for him to get his nerves up to say what was really in his heart.

Swallowing the last drop of his nervousness, he said, "I want to marry you. Will you marry me, Teresa?"

Roger and Courtney returned home and received the shock of their lives. Mrs. Williams and Dr. Palmer were engaged to be married.

One month later, they had a private wedding with only close family members in attendance. They sailed to the Bahamas for their honeymoon and sent everyone a post card once they arrived on the magical island.

One night when her family was sleeping, Courtney got up and finished her collage. She put in her cassette by Surface to hear one of her favorite songs titled "Shower Me With Your Love," while cutting out many pictures for this special collage.

Taking the tape in her hand, she began laying out her pictures to format. She took a picture of Roger, Lil' Roger, and one of herself to place in the middle. Then she found a nice picture of her parents from their younger days together. Next, she found a picture of Roger's parents and placed it next to hers. She even included a picture of Stanley that she had received from Dr. Palmer.

Courtney then cut out several pictures of her sisters, brothers-in-law, nieces, and nephews. In this collage, she had pictures of everyone related to her. Some were featured more than once since she had lots of space to be filled.

She even put a picture of the deceased Steven in this collage right at the top. Now that Courtney's collage was complete, she felt a sense of peace as she hung it on the wall in the living room for Roger to see.

All of the anxieties she'd faced in her life were hanging on the living room wall. They wouldn't trouble her anymore. She felt that her life was complete and her collage showed it better than she ever could.

"So, Roger, what do you think?" she asked when he quietly entered the living room.

"I think it's beautiful. It's Courtney's Collage."

The end

About the Author

Sherille Fisher was born and raised in a small community in Miami, Florida, called Richmond Heights. She lived within walking distance of her grandmother Drewcilla, her aunts, uncles and many cousins. She was brought up in the church, where she gained a fondness for music at an early age and began singing in the choir at age seven. She graduated from Miami South Ridge High School. In 1983 she went to Houston, Texas to visit her first cousin, Gilda, and her husband, Thomas. She met her future husband, Harrison Fisher Sr., in church the very next day.

Sherille and Harrison have been married twenty-four years and they have five children: Kelley, Dominique, Harrison, Jr., Jacob, and Joshua. She and her family moved to Tallahassee, Florida, in 2000; then relocated back to Houston, Texas in 2005 where they presently reside. She enjoyed working in the medical field for a number of years as a Certified Nursing Assistant, and is now employed in the retail industry. She and her family attend Covenant Glen United Methodist Church, where she sings in the choir and enjoys singing just as much as writing.

Sherille's short story, *Nothing in Common*, was published in the *How I Met My Sweetheart Anthology* (February 2007).

E-mail: Fisherlawhrf@aol.com

About the Author

Barbara Joe-Williams was born and raised in Rosston, Arkansas. She is a former business school teacher, guidance counselor, and reading instructor. She's a graduate of Tallahassee Community College and Florida A&M University.

Currently, she is a freelance writer and an independent publisher living in Tallahassee, Florida. She spends her spare time traveling as a motivational teacher or conducting workshops on writing, publishing, and marketing. She has successfully published several books for herself and a list of titles for other aspiring authors.

Other titles available from this author include:

A Writer's Guide to Self-Publishing and Marketing, 03/07
How I Met My Sweetheart (Anthology), 02/07
Falling for Lies, 10/06
Dancing with Temptation, 11/05
Forgive Us This Day, 11/04

Blog: http://Blog.myspace.com/Barbarajoewilliams
E-mail: Amanipublishing@aol.com
Website: www.Amanipublishing.net

Printed in the United States
200123BV00008B/265-273/A